HALF

DEMON

RENEE JOINER

Oshun
Publications

Half Demon © 2020 by Renee Joiner
ISBN: 978-1-950378-34-0

Book Design by Msvicki's Designs
www.allcoverbookdesigns.com

Published by Oshun Publications
www.oshunpublications.com

Contents

Other Books by Renee

Thorne Sisters Chronicles

Possessed by Magic

Reincarnated by Magic

Immortal by Magic

.

.

Did you know you can take every story with you?

I know it's tough these days to simply find the time to relax and curl up with a good book. This is why I'm delighted to share that I have books available in audio book format.

Best of all, you can get the audio book version of any book by me for free as part of a 30-day Audible trial.

Members get free audio books every month and exclusive discounts. It's an excellent way to explore and determine if audio book learning works for you.

If you're not satisfied, you can cancel anytime within the trial period. You won't be charged, and you can even keep your audio book.

To choose a free audio book, click on your favorite title's cover to be taken to Audible's website for details.

Remember, there's no obligation to buy.

reneejoinerauthor.com/audiobooks

JOIN MY
NEWSLETTER

GET UPDATES,
FREEBIES & GIVEAWAYS

RENEEJOINERAUTHOR.COM/NEWSLETTER

Darkness Is My Friend

IT'S BEEN SEVERAL MONTHS NOW SINCE I WOKE UP IN THAT hospital bed, and they told me my name was Jane Doe. I didn't know anything. I had so many memories, but none of them made sense. There were only two things I was sure about; my name is Reese, not Jane Doe, and I have to kill Durin. I don't know who he is or why I hate him. All I know is his name and that I want him to die no matter what. I'm willing to do anything and everything in my power to make sure that happens.

I pulled the hood from my head as I watched his men go about their business. They were moving boxes from a shipping crate to a parked van on the road nearby. I don't care what's in the boxes. I don't care why they're doing this. I just care about getting to Durin, and to do that, I need to make one of them talk.

I've been working my way up the chain of power, and these guys aren't exactly important, but they're the closest I've gotten to him. According to the last guy I killed, these boxes get delivered directly to the big guy. One of these guys knows precisely where he is.

Beating them and overpowering them would be easy, even though I'm only 5'2 and have a slender build. I'm all muscle and power, no matter how small I look. Getting them to talk, that is going to be the hard part. Durin's guys are as loyal as an old dog is to a good owner. Everyone has their breaking point, though, and I'm going to find one of theirs.

First things first, single one of them out and separate him from the group. They lose all of their confidence and will to fight when they're helpless and alone. I can't risk alerting all of them. One of them may run back to Durin and warn him. Then he'll move his operation, and I'll have to start from the beginning again. I've worked too hard and come too far to be set back like that. I have to be careful and work slowly. Luckily I've learned how to use the shadows to my advantage.

I pulled my hood back up and jumped down from my hiding spot on the roof. It's a three-story building, but I land on the floor as silent as a leaf falling from a tree. My skinny jeans and cotton hoody were tight against my skin and pitch black. They should help me blend in with the shadows and move quickly. The jeans, while tight and stuck to my skin, were stretchy too, which helped me move around freely. I need that extra freedom, especially when I get into a fight. A leather jacket looked cooler, but the cotton hoody is quiet and comfortable.

I made my way through the graveyard of shipping containers. The air was still, and the sky clear. The cold light from the crescent moon threatened to expose me as I tried my best to avoid it. There wasn't a lot of darkness to work with, but there was enough for me to get close to Durin's men.

I came up beside the shipping container and climbed up on top of it. I laid my body flat against the metal and hoped none of them were curious enough to look up. I pulled my body toward the open doors and peered over the edge. I looked down at them as they each grabbed a box and carried it off the truck. They weren't close to each other, but they were still in sight of one another. If I grabbed one here, the rest of them would surely see. I need to wait. One of them will break off from the others, and then I can seize my chance.

I waited for a while. I wasn't keeping track of time, so I'm not sure how long. The container was half empty, and the van had driven off only to be replaced by another. Then it finally happened.

"Hey, where do you think you're going?" One of the men shouted at the other, who was creeping off toward the maze of shipping containers.

"I'm going to take a leak! Do you mind, or maybe you want to come and watch," the man replied to the one that seemed to be in charge.

The one who is in charge hissed and waved for him to go, "Just make it quick."

I tried to contain my excitement, but a grin pushed its way onto my face. This is it. This is my chance to get to Durin. I scurried off the top of the shipping container and made my way around the rest of the containers. I needed to catch up with him quickly before I lost sight of him, and it's all over. I can't see anything from down here, so I jumped up onto one of the containers and leaped from one to the other. I caught sight of him and then leaped back down to the ground.

I waited in the shadows while he relieved himself all over the side of a wall. I don't feel like attacking a man in the middle of his piss, so I'll just wait till he is finished. He shook off and zipped his pants up. It's action time. I stepped out of the shadows and pushed my hood off my head as I got into my fighting stance. The man turned around and gasped when he saw me. First, he was shocked, then I saw confusion flash past his eyes, then his eyes burned with anger, and a smile meant to pity me spread across his face.

"What the hell do you think you're doing here, girl?" the man asked in a gruff voice. "Go on home before I make you regret coming out tonight."

"I'm not going anywhere tonight, except to Durin's hiding place," I responded, keeping my voice low and confident to show that he didn't scare me. "You're going to tell me exactly where I can find Durin, and then as a reward, I'll give you a quick and painless death. Well, kind of painless."

The man stood still and stayed silent for a while. Slowly his eyes widened, and his mouth opened up wide. He let out a loud and bellowing laugh. He leaned over, placing his one hand on his knee and cradling his shaking belly with the other. I stayed where I was, crossed my arms over my chest, and waited for him to finish. They always do this when they see me. They think, 'oh no, it's a little girl. She's going to beat me up and kill me.' Then they laugh at the little joke they made in their head. When they're done laughing they get serious and promise me I'm going to regret every decision I've ever made in my life. That's usually when the fighting starts. I waited patiently for that moment.

The man's face hardened, and his laughter trailed off into silence, "Now girl, enough games. Let me show you exactly just how much trouble you've gotten yourself into."

I smiled and whispered, "Finally."

His hands moved fast to grab his gun, currently hidden in the loop of his belt by the small of his back, but I can move more quickly. I darted toward him, only a blur to his eyes. I grabbed his hand and twisted it behind him, pushing his hand into the middle of his back. Then I braced my other hand against his shoulder and pushed his upper body over. I forced his body to lean forward.

"What the hell!" He cried out, realizing he failed his attempt to intimidate and possibly kill me.

"Now, have I made my point, or do I have to cause you an incredibly enormous amount of pain before you tell me where Durin is?" I couldn't help but smile at my ability to kick men like this down a few steps. Men like him will always underestimate and mistreat women until you give him a reason to tuck his tail between his legs.

He struggled to look back at me, but when he saw my face, his eyes widened, but not with fear. He was surprised.

"Hey, what the hell are you doing," he spat. "This isn't funny, Reese, let me go!"

Wait, what? He knows my name. I couldn't help it. I let him go. I was shocked for a moment. I let him go, but I made sure to grab his gun and pull it away from him first. Don't want him getting the upper hand just because he surprised me.

I point the gun directly at his head and keep my finger soft against the trigger. "Who are you, and how the hell do you know my name?"

"Stop playing around, Reese. You're going to break your cover. Get out of here before someone sees you." The man seemed genuine when he spoke. He genuinely looked as if he was worried for me and concerned.

"Answer my question," I stood my ground and redirected the gun at his knee, "or I'll pull the trigger."

"You've gone mad!" He put his hands over his knee as if that would make a difference when I shot it. "Seriously, what's your deal?"

I just keep getting more confused. This man seems to

genuinely know who I am, and he is really confused by why I'm acting this way. That can't be, though. He is one of Durin's men. How could he know me? I hate Durin, and I don't know why, but it must have something to do with what happened to me in my past life. The life I lived before I woke up in that hospital bed.

"Who am I?" I asked the man, but this made him raise his eyebrows. "Who am I to you?" I repeated.

"Is this a joke?" He stood up straight, forgetting that I had his gun pointed at his knee. "If this is a joke, then I've got to tell you it's not a very good one. You shouldn't pursue a career in comedy."

"I have no plans too, now answer my question!" I'm out of patience. My finger tightens around the trigger, and I'm seconds away from pulling it.

Before I can, we're interrupted. The men must have heard our yelling because they've dropped their boxes, and they've come running to their colleague's rescue. They pile into the small part of the shipping yard we're standing in. I spot one of them, the one that's in charge, reaching for his gun. I pulled my gun away from the man I was talking to and pointed it at him. His gun was already out and pointed directly at my head. This could be the end of it.

I cursed myself for letting my guard down like this. We will pull the triggers at the same time, and it's all up to whose aim is better. After all these months, I can't believe it's going to end like this.

He pulled the trigger, but before I could pull mine, someone jumped in front of me, and the bullet that was meant to hit me sunk into his chest. His body dropped to the floor. I looked down at the man who I was just threatening with his own gun as his blood pooled on the floor by my feet.

Why would he do that? Why would he sacrifice himself

for me? The other men were shocked, and I took the opportunity to regain the upper hand.

Guns were useless weapons to me. They only worked for intimidation. I threw the gun in my hand at the man in charge. It smacked him in the face and made him drop his own gun in order to cradle his face. I rushed forward, and once again, I was too fast for them to see. I slid my foot across the floor, kicking both guns away, and then I twisted my body and lifted my other foot. I spun my whole body into the kick as the heel of my foot collided with the man's face the moment he removed his hands. He cursed out loud and flipped over backward.

The moment their boss hit the floor, the rest of the men converged on me. Usually, four on one would be unfair, but I can move so fast that none of them will know what hit them.

One of them reached out to pull my hair. I spun around, grabbed his hand, and twisted his wrist. Before he could cry out from the pain, I brought my elbow up and smacked it against his chin. His mouth was open, so that made him slam his teeth shut on his tongue. I immediately turned my attention to the next man, lifting his leg up to kick me in the stomach. I turned around just in time to grab his leg and push it into the man next to him. I then grabbed the back of both their heads and slammed their faces into one another.

The last man was easy. I moved so fast that all he saw was a blur, and then his colleagues were left on the floor moaning and cursing, except for the one who bit his tongue. He was on his knees, crying, but too much blood was coming out of his mouth for him to talk.

The last man froze in place and looked around at the carnage I had made. I decided to go to plan B. This man must know something or else he wouldn't be working this operation. I'll have to take him and get whatever information I can.

I took one step forward, and before he knew what was happening, I was behind him with my arm wrapped around his neck. He squirmed and clawed at my arm, but I held on tight. These men might be strong to other women, but I'm not like any woman they've ever met. In these past months, after waking up from the hospital, I haven't met anyone who can match my strength and speed yet. To me, these men are like toddlers screaming in their cribs.

Soon the man stopped squirming, and his body went limp in my arms. I lift his body and drape him across my shoulders. I might have resembled a monster, with his huge muscular body on top of my slim frame. He wasn't too heavy for me, though. I looked at the rest of the men, but I was sure they wouldn't follow me. They were too busy licking their wounds. I should have enough time to interrogate him. Maybe then my search for Durin will finally be over.

2

Interrogation Attempt

I COULDN'T TAKE THE MAN TOO FAR AWAY. I NEEDED TO GET him somewhere secure, so we could talk without interruption, but if I took too long, then one of the other men could inform Durin. He would be gone from his hiding place before I have a chance to get to him. I needed to act quickly. There was a building nearby, so I took the man there. All I had to do was break down the door and tie him to a chair. Usually, I would try splashing some water on his face to wake him up. Still, since there was no source of water for me to use, I raised my hand, pulled it as far back as my shoulder joint would allow, and then brought it down with all of my fury across his face.

The slap woke the man up so hard that he tried to jump up out of the chair. The rope I found and used to tie him down stopped him from jumping up too far. The chair did move a bit, which impressed me.

"You're not going anywhere, so I suggest you stop flapping around like a fish and answer some of my questions," I want to be austere. I've watched a few movies, and my favorite part is always when the villain is interrogating the heroes, or they're allies. Not that I see myself as a villain, but I do enjoy standing half in the shadows at the corner of the room so that all my victims can see is my sly smile.

"You better cut the crap right now, Reese," the man spoke. He sounded angry but also confused, and I detected a hint of fear. "You're in way over your head. How could you attack us on a night like this?"

I listened to him, but in the back of my mind, all I could hear were cuckoo clocks. This guy is mad.

"You need to cut the crap!" I started my bad cop routine. "Tell me everything you know about Durin. I need details! Tell me where his hideout is, tell me how to get close to him. Talk!" I rushed out of my shadows and leaned forward till our faces were only inches apart. I bared my teeth and breathed hot air on his cheek. I saw someone do this on a show once, and it really worked.

"Why are you asking me questions you already know the answers to? Is this some kind of test? Is Durin testing me?"

"Stop messing around! Give me at least one answer," my interrogation isn't going as well as the ones in the movies. Usually, the victim starts talking by now. Maybe I should try being a good cop. "Listen, I'm not the bad guy here. I'm your friend, and friends help each other. Right? You scratch my back, and I'll scratch yours." I should start with more straightforward questions then move on to the hard ones. "What was in those boxes you guys were moving out there?"

"Durin doesn't tell us what's in the boxes, you know that. He's more likely to tell you what's in the boxes rather than us."

Now I'm getting annoyed and even more confused. Why the hell would Durin be more likely to tell me what's in the boxes? This guy must just be poking at my nerves to see how easily I'll crack. That's not going to happen. I'll break him in half before I let him get to me like that.

I kept my calm and continued with the questions.

"Not that you answered my last question, but let's move on to the next one, shall we? Just so we can feel productive. Where are the boxes being taken?"

"You should know. You know very well that only the driver knows where the vans go. You should have kidnapped him."

"Stop saying that I know things when I don't!" I might have lost my cool, and I might not be doing the good cop routine. "And stop pretending you know me because you don't. Tell me where Durin is now!"

I slammed my hands down on the arms of the chair, and he managed to move his hands out the way just in time. He leaned back in the chair, and I could see the fear finally showing in his eyes.

"You've gone mad. You've gone proper mad, haven't you," he cried, and the fear was pretty clear in his voice as well. "Come on, Reese, wake up! Stop acting like this."

"You're the one that needs to stop acting. I know you're higher up on the chain of command than you're letting on. Durin doesn't let any of his normal goons handle goods like you were handling tonight. Durin trusts you. You know where those boxes are going, and you know they're going straight to Durin. You better tell me now, or I'm going to start removing a few of your attachments, and by attachments, I mean fingers, toes, your tongue, you know those kinds of things."

Maybe that threat will be enough to get his lips moving more favorably. These people don't know me, and the playing dumb act gets boring really quickly. He looked at me for a moment, probably trying to see if I have the guts to back up my threat. Trust me, I do. He opened his mouth to speak, but before he could say anything, we were interrupted by the sound of a door opening behind us.

"Shit, the cavalry's here," I muttered.

I knew this was taking too long. The men I let go got themselves up and went to fetch help. They probably ran back to mommy with their tails between their legs. I hate people like that. I turned to face the men that Durin sent as backup, and then I saw his face.

One man was leading them. He was standing in front and leading the way while the rest of the men followed. I know him. I don't know how, but I know him. He is the most familiar thing I have seen since I woke up in the hospital all those months ago. The only thing I knew then was my name and Durin's, but now I know this man. I know his face, and I think I know him, but I'm not sure.

The man tied to the chair behind me was glad to see the man.

"Ethan! It's about time," he said.

That's his name then, Ethan. The name matches the face. I know they belong together, but I still don't know who he is. He was looking around. He looked at the man tied to the chair, and then he looked at me. He had a scowl on his face, but as his dark blue eyes caught mine, his face lit up. A smile slowly spread across his face. It was a confused but happy smile.

"Reese! Oh my god, Reese, you're alive!" Ethan exclaimed, his smile growing wider the longer he looked at me. "What the hell are you doing here?"

"She doesn't remember," the man tied to the chair yelled at him. "She's acting like she doesn't know anything. She doesn't know me, and she probably doesn't know you. She put me in this chair, Goddamnit!"

Ethan looked back and forth between the man in the chair and me. He looked at me with new eyes. These eyes were questioning me, but for some reason, they still trusted me.

"Reese is that true?" he took a step toward me, and I took a step back. "Reese, do you not remember him? Do you not remember me?"

He kept walking forward, but with each step he took toward me, I took a step away from him. He was acting as if I was a wild animal, and he was trying to calm me down. If you want to calm down a wild animal, you shouldn't back it into a corner. The other men started to surround me, but he gestured for them to stay back.

"Reese, look at me," he spoke softly, and for some reason, his voice made me feel safe. "I'm not here to hurt you. Things may seem a bit odd right now, but you have to believe me when I say that I'm not your enemy. We are not your enemy."

He took one more step forward, and I stepped back. My heel stepped on something. I glanced back over my shoulder. The man tied to the chair was right behind me, and I had just stepped on his foot. I looked around me, and it seemed like I had nowhere to go. I was trapped. That's their mistake, though, because a trapped animal is far more dangerous than a free one.

I positioned my body for the fight to come. Before I could do anything, the man behind me stood up and ripped his arms free of the rope that was binding him to the chair. He kicked the chair away. I tried to turn to face him, but he caught me by surprise. He grabbed both my wrists and pulled my arms back. All I needed to do was flex my arms, and I would break free, but before I could do that, Ethan rushed toward me, and everything went black.

3

Different

It was dark, and there was a throbbing pain at the back of my head. I could hear voices around me, but I couldn't make out any words they were saying. All the noises around me melted together. I tried to open my eyes slowly. I didn't want to let anyone around me know that I'm awake, but I also don't like being in the dark. I want to see what's happening, so I know what my next move needs to be.

There was very little light in the room, but the light that was there was blinding. I blinked a couple times to get used to it. Once the blur was gone, I had a look around. My eyes darted from one side of the room to the other. I was lying on my side on the floor. There was nothing but a wall in front of me, and all the voices were coming from behind me.

"I want to know what the hell is going on here," I heard a familiar voice say. It sounded like the man they called Ethan talking. "This isn't part of the plan. How can she not remember, and how did she manage to take you guys down? There were five of you. I know she's good, but she's not that good."

They were whispering as if they didn't want to wake me. Too late for that, I guess.

"I know just as much as you do," another voice replied. "All I know is that she was fast, incredibly fast, and strong. Stronger and faster than any human should be."

They're distracted, I have to make my move now, or I'll be lying on the floor until they make up their minds on what they're going to do with me. I slowly moved my head around so I could glance behind me. There were only two of them, Ethan and the man I tied to the chair. The other men that were here must have left already. I glanced around the room quickly. This room was different from the one I was in before everything went black.

Shit, they must have moved me while I was out. Now I have no idea where I am, and I'm practically at these guys' mercy. That's not a problem, though. I've been in worse situations, and I can always fight my way out of it. Now is as good a time as ever to start the fighting part.

I spin onto my stomach and push myself up onto my feet. The men were so busy talking that they noticed me too late. Ethan was further away from me than the other one was. He wasn't the immediate threat. I leaped toward the closer man. He turned to counterattack me, but he was too slow now like he was too slow when I first knocked him out. I didn't want to kill him, but I didn't want to fight two men at once. I needed to get rid of him quickly so that the only one left to fight was Ethan.

I lifted my arms up on either side of his head and slammed my hands together against his ears. He cried out and folded forward from the pain. As his head went down, I brought my knee up to meet his face. That shot him back up, and as a final measure, I slammed my curled fist in between his ribs. He grunted as the wind got knocked out of him and then fell to the ground. I did that all in about 30 seconds. It seems like the more I fight, the faster I get.

I turned to face Ethan. He could have moved toward me by now, but he stayed where he was. He didn't look shocked or angry. He just stood there and stared at me as if he was trying to answer a question in his mind.

"I've spent quite a few months now tracking down Durin's men and tearing them down," I decided to start the conversation because I know how much Durin's men love to talk. "You're the first one to move fast enough to knock me out like that. I'm impressed."

"I'm also impressed," he replied. "You're a lot faster and stronger than you were the last time I saw you. You're trained to be fast and strong, but there's only so much you can do as a human. That is unless you're not human anymore."

This guy is crazier than the rest of them, but he knows me, or he knew who I used to be. He seems high up in Durin's chain of command, higher than any of the men I've interrogated. I could get some answers from him. All I have to do is keep him talking.

He rushes toward me, almost too fast for me to react. I had less than a second to move out the way. As I moved to counter him, he moved again to counter me. We were like blurry lines in the room, dashing from one corner to the next, trying to avoid each other. With every move he made toward me, I moved away. I was fast, but this guy seemed like he could match my speed perfectly. That's enough games. He can match my speed, but can he match my strength and power.

He moved toward me again, but this time I didn't move away. This time I was ready to take him on. I kept my palm open and straight so that my nails were extended out. I thrust my arm out at him, and my hand acted like a knife slicing through the air. He saw it coming just in time and turned his body away from the attack. He was fast but not fast enough. My fingernails sliced his cheek, leaving a tiny tear in the skin. A drop of blood squeezed out of the cut.

The cut didn't seem to bother him because he didn't even pause to notice it. He immediately came at me with a counterattack. He kept his hands curled into a fist as he threw a punch at my shoulder. I managed to deflect his attack by turning my shoulder out of his reach and slapping my extended hand's side into his wrist, swiping his fist to the side.

That was just the start of the fight. Soon we were swiping, slicing, kicking, and punching at each other. We each moved too fast for the other, and neither one of us was able to land a blow on the other. We attacked and counterattacked. He matched my strength and speed, and I matched his. No matter how fast I moved, he could move just as fast. No matter how hard I hit, he could hit just as hard. Not that we actually managed to hit one another. He deflected my attacks, and I deflected his.

"What are you doing here, Reese?" he asked me while he pushed one of my kicks away.

"Isn't it obvious?" I replied while bending backward to avoid a punch to the face. "I'm looking for Durin, and either you or one of your men are going to tell me where he is."

"You're off mission Reese," he continued, completely ignoring my reply and deflecting another slice from my nails. "You being here is dangerous. You could blow your cover and put yourself and the whole mission in jeopardy."

I jumped as he swiped his legs sideways by my feet. In the split second I hovered in the air I shot my own kick at his face, but he blocked it with his forearm. This man knows something about me, but I'm torn between getting answers about my past and getting answers about Durin. I landed on the ground just as he pushed himself back up. The battle and the interrogation continued.

"If you know so much about me, then you should know why I want to know where Durin is," I bargained with him. "Tell me how to find him, and then I'll get back to this mission you think is so important."

"You already know where Durin is," he pushed my fist away from his face and countered with a kick that I jumped away from. "This isn't you, Reese. I know how you fight, and this isn't how you fight. You're too angry, and you're not thinking about the end game. That's not how you fight."

"Stop acting like you know me and just answer my question."

Neither one of use has landed a blow on the other yet. I keep attacking, and he keeps dodging or deflecting. He keeps attacking, and I keep dodging and deflecting. It seems as though he is my match in every way, or is he? The one thing I haven't shown him yet is my power. He's seen my speed and has matched it, he's seen my strength and has matched it. He hasn't seen my ability, and I haven't seen his.

"Tell me, Reese, who put you up to this? Who put you on Durin's path and told you to pursue him like this?"

Reese rolled her eyes, just like a man to assume there's someone else standing behind a woman. To assume that she is being controlled or directed rather than thinking, she has thoughts and desires of her own to pursue.

"No one!" I growled at him. "I'm out for Durin because I need to stop him. I need to kill him. No one else but myself has put me on this path."

I extended my hand again and attempted to swipe at his chest. He curled his hand into a fist and tried to punch my chest. Our forearms collided, and we blocked each other. I pushed my arm into his, and he pushed back. We were locked in a stalemate. Either one of us could break it by moving our free arm forward for a counterattack, but neither one of us did that. Our arms shook as we pushed into each other. I stared up at him, and he stared back.

I've never seen eyes so dark. I've never seen such a deep blue. It was almost as if his eyes were black in this light. His eyes were full of emotion. The emotion in his eyes was different than the emotion on his face. His face showed anger and focus, but his eyes showed concern and love. Was it love for me? It couldn't be. I don't even know who he is, and no matter how much he tries to convince me that he knows me, he doesn't. Even if he knew me in the past, I'm a different person now, and he can't change that.

A loud bang, followed by yelling and shouting, broke our concentration. We pulled away from each other and turned our attention in the direction of the new noise.

"They're here!" Ethan growled and cursed underneath his breath. He turned back to me with fear in his eyes. "You need to get out of here. They can't see you here, or it will all be over. Just stay low and keep yourself out of trouble until I can find you again. I have your scent now, so I will find you again."

I opened my mouth to reply. I wasn't sure what I was going to say, but I don't like it when people try to tell me what to do. Before I could say anything, he ran off. He left me alone in the room with the unconscious man. The sounds were getting louder, which meant that whoever was out there was getting closer. Someone found us alright, but it wasn't anyone I knew, and judging by Ethan's reaction, they weren't on his side either.

I did what he said, not because he said it but because I was done fighting for the night. It was difficult, but I found my way out of the building, and I got as far away from it as possible. I don't know who Ethan is, but he knows who I am. All this time, the only thought on my mind was getting to Durin, but now I had a new goal. I'm going to find out who I was in my past, and Ethan is going to help me.

4

Three Tails

THE POPCORN IS TOO SALTY, AND THE SODA IS ICED DOWN so much if I ordered water; instead, it would have tasted the same. That didn't matter, though. The only reason I ordered the snacks was so I could fit in better. The best way to follow someone is to blend in with the crowd around them, which is why I'm wearing blue, worn shorts, and a pink shirt with a fox on it instead of dressing in all black. That's usually how people dress on a hot day out at the carnival.

Ethan wasn't dressed like that. He wore dark blue, denim jeans, a gray t-shirt, and a denim jacket to match his jeans. He has a good fashion sense, I'll give him that. He knows just the right shirt to wear to advertise and define his abs and biceps. That's enough admiration. I need to concentrate on what he's doing. I didn't spend the last week following him, learning his habits, and memorizing his routes just to gush over his muscles and wardrobe.

I leaned against one of the vendors and watched him from a distance. My eyes allow me to see farther than the average human eye. I stood a staggering 50 feet away from him, and I could see perfectly. I always make an effort to stay no more or less than 50 feet away from the people I'm tracking. That's far enough to be able to see and hear whatever I need to, but too far for him to pick up my scent. That is if he's not looking for it. A demon's sense of smell is both his strongest and his weakest sense.

He's waiting, and I'm not sure what for. I'm prepared to wait just as long as he is. All I have to do is lie low, keep out of his sight, and keep quiet. If I speak, I risk him hearing my voice and recognizing it. I assume he can see just as far as I can, if not further. I haven't met anyone who could outmaneuver me the way he did. I'm sure he has other talents he's keeping hidden.

I moved from my spot to the next vendor and ordered some cotton candy. It's better to keep moving if you don't want the person you're following to notice you. No one else is just standing in the background staring at him, so I can't do that either. I have to act natural. I pulled a piece of my pink cotton candy off and let it melt in my mouth. That was when I smelt her.

I caught her scent a few days ago, and it keeps popping up around me. She's following me. That I know for sure. I glanced around to see if I could spot her, but I didn't want to make it obvious that I was looking for someone. I've seen her face in passing a few times. I knew about the third time I saw her that I had developed a tail.

There she is. I finally spot her sitting down on a bench across the way from me. She tried hard not to look my way, but it's evident that she was looking at me. If she was tailing anyone else, she would probably be doing a good job. Too bad she chose to tail me, and I'm not only good at tailing other people, I'm also good at spotting a tail. It was made easy for me because of my strong sense.

This was the first time since she started following me

that I could get a good look at her. Her hair stretched past her shoulders and near the small of her back. It was tied up in a high pony. If she let her hair loose, it would probably reach past her butt. It was the darkest auburn brown I have ever seen. Her hair looked like the bark of a tree. Even from here, I could see her eye color. They were also dark brown. They were mesmerizing in a way as if there was some deep dark secret hidden behind them.

I couldn't help but stare, but I made sure to keep myself out of her sight. She was strangely beautiful. It wasn't your normal modern beauty you see on the streets these days. It was a natural and fierce beauty. There wasn't even a hint of makeup on her face, and she wasn't dressed to show off her breasts or her butt and yet she was still more attractive than the women wearing low cleavage V-necks and short skirts. I liked her. In some way, I didn't mind having her tail me, as long as she didn't get in the way of my mission.

I realized I had been focused on her for too long. My head snapped back in Ethan's direction, but he wasn't there anymore.

"Shit," I cursed underneath my breath.

I didn't want to look panicked, but I needed to find him. I needed to follow his scent. I made my way over to the last place I saw him and hoped that his scent was still there. I picked up his scent, but it was weak. He must have moved off a while ago.

"Damn it!" I was too busy admiring some women who's been tailing me to notice that my tail walked off without me.

Did Ethan know I was here? Was this woman working with him? Was it his plan to distract me long enough so he could escape? I refused to believe that he could fool me that easily. It must just be bad luck for me and good luck for him.

I can't follow his scent when it's this week, so I'll have to let him go today. At least I know his habits and routine. I know exactly where I can find him tomorrow. That means all I need to do for the rest of the day is lose my tail and go home.

I HAD to wake up early. In the few weeks, I've been following Ethan I've learned that he likes to get the day started before the sun has even risen. That means I have to wake up before him and get to the coffee shop where he usually starts his day.

I watched him order his usual double-shot Irish coffee with mint sprinkled over the cream. He has weird taste in coffee, but I was here to watch and not judge. He only waited for about 2 minutes every morning. As if they knew he was coming. I watched from the rooftop of the next building as he took the coffee, drunk it in one gulp, and continued with his day.

He usually met a lot of people during his walk down the streets, but today was different. I jumped from rooftop to rooftop as I watched him walk right past all of his usual contacts. They would step forward and ask him a stupid question, but he would just shake his head and keep going. This was strange. He wasn't following his routine, and that worried me.

Perhaps he did spot me yesterday and is now playing his cards close to his chest. I carried on and refused to believe that he knew I was following him. I'm good at what I do, and I haven't been made yet.

The day dragged as he continued to ignore his usual

contacts and do the strangest things. I watched him go into a grocery store and buy a loaf of bread. Then he carried the bread to the nearest pond and started crumbling it on the ground for the pigeons. Now I'm convinced he knows I'm watching him, or perhaps he thinks that someone else is following him.

I took my eyes off of him for the first time today and looked around. I scanned the area as far away as my eyes would allow me to while still seeing clearly. I spotted the same woman that's been tailing me sitting on a bench on the other side of the park. It's not hard to imagine that if I've spotted her before, then so has Ethan. He might be keeping his cards close to his chest because of her, but he's never done that before. There must be something going on. I kept scanning the area. Ethan wouldn't let himself be scared off by a human woman, so there's got to be someone else out there that he's worried about.

I spotted him. Everyone else in the park looks human and smells human, but this man doesn't have a smell. A man with no scent can only be a demon I haven't met yet. I studied his face and tried to remember if I had seen it somewhere else today, but I haven't. I wasn't looking out for other faces. He was standing close to Ethan. He's closer to Ethan than me or the other woman is. He must be the reason that Ethan's been acting so strange all day long.

I let out a sigh accidentally. Once I realized, I checked to see Ethan didn't hear me. He continued throwing bread to the birds, so he must not have. I can't abandon him now. I'll just have to wait until he can shake this new tail and lead me to the man I'm looking for.

It's starting to get boring, and I force down a yawn. Eventually, Ethan gets up and leaves the park. I wait before following him. I keep my eyes on the man to see if he walks after Ethan, and he does. He paused only a few moments before following. Great, now I need to follow Ethan, avoid the man following him, and avoid the woman following me. Could this get any more difficult? In any case, I've invested too much in this to let it go.

I wait for both of them to get to a comfortable distance before following after them. Ethan walked down the street a little faster now. It's as if he confirmed his tail, and he's eager to get rid of it. I'm just glad that someone else managed to get themselves made by him and not me. I followed them both for another four blocks, and my tail followed me closely.

Jumping from rooftop to rooftop is getting tiring. I dropped down in an alleyway and then followed it to the next block to catch up with Ethan and his tail. As I came to the end of the alley, I let the shadows hide me in my all black clothing, and I peeked my head out to spy on them. I watched as Ethan disappeared into some building. The building looked old and abandoned, but not yet falling apart. The man tailing him waited for a few moments as if he was hesitating. Still, he eventually followed Ethan into the building.

I stepped out from the alleyway and into the light. I can't follow them in there. My only option is to wait here for one of them to come out. My guess is that Ethan is leading him to lose him or deal with him. Either way, I'm sure only one of them will come out eventually.

Now may be the perfect time for me to deal with my own tail.

5

Marisa

I stood up and disappeared back into the alleyway. I knew the woman was watching me from behind the nearby building. As I sank into the alley, I quickly dug my nails into the surface of the bricks and climbed back up to the roof. I watched her from there. She walked closer, glancing around constantly, hoping she wasn't spotted by anyone. She peered into the dark alleyway she saw me go into, but at that moment, I was right on top of her.

She looked up as I dropped down and landed on the floor in front of her. She jumped back, but she obviously knew there was no point in running away. Her eyes were wide, not with disbelief but with fear.

"Can I help you?" I asked her, keeping my voice low and intimidating, although my question was a bit cliché.

"I-I-I-," she stuttered and took a few more steps back. "How long have you known I was following you?"

"Since you started," I replied, although it's a lie. She was probably following me for a few days before I first noticed her. It took me two days after that to realize that she was tailing me. "I'm sure you have an excellent reason for following me around. Now would be the time to tell me what it is."

I saw the fear slowly leave her eyes as she realized that I wasn't going to hurt her. I'm not the type of person to hurt people without reason. I like to ask questions first. She stood up with a bit more strength and pride in her step and looked straight at me. Now I can see the determination in her eyes.

"I wasn't sure if you were the right person," she started explaining, "but after seeing you jump from rooftop to rooftop, the way you move with agility, speed, and strength, you must be her."

I'm not entirely sure if she is actually constructing complete sentences or if she is babbling one.

"I must be who?"

"You must be the vigilante who's been going around the city and killing off all of those gang members."

I let out a sigh. I've been dealing with Durin's men for months now. It was only a matter of time before someone noticed me. He does run one of the biggest gangs on this side of the city. The police have been chasing the mysterious vigilante, but they don't know that I'm a woman. They still believe that only a strong and powerful man can do what I've been doing. This woman must be smarter than I thought she was if she knows more than the police do.

"Why have you been looking for me?" I asked, stepping closer. "What does someone like you have to do with this gang?"

"I don't have anything to do with them," she replied, and I listened carefully to her heartbeat to see if she was lying. Humans can't help it. When they lie, their hearts go wild, and it's very easy to tell. "A couple of weeks ago, you saved a young girl. Those men had surrounded her in an alleyway, and I'm sure they were seconds away from having their way with her. You dropped down from the rooftop, beat them all up, and then you let her go. You told her to run and get help. She did exactly that, but you were gone by the time she came back with the police, and the men were all dead."

Her heartbeat remained steady, and her voice didn't crack as she spoke. She was telling the truth.

"That young girl wasn't you," I told her. I remember that night. She was maybe 16 or 17 years old, lying in a puddle of tears on the floor with bruises all over her. Those men were animals, and I don't even want to think about what they would have done if I wasn't there. "Why does it matter to you that I helped the girl?"

"She was my sister," tears welled up in her eyes and her voice cracked from holding them back. "You saved my sister, and I needed to know if it was you. I needed to know if you were the right person to thank."

My heart felt a little warm and fuzzy. No one has ever thanked me. Not that I'm out there looking for people to thank me. It would be nice every now and again. I fought a smile and kept my face blank and detached from the situation.

"I don't ask to be thanked, and I don't need to be," I told her. "I do what I do for my own reasons. Those men were monsters in more ways than one, and they needed to be taken care of."

I stepped closer to her and began to circle. I felt like a predator examining my prey, but I couldn't help myself. I've only ever seen her from a distance, and she's always intrigued me. Now I get a closer look, and I can't help but be excited.

Her body was slim but built, like a runner's or swimmer's body. She keeps herself in shape, but she doesn't go overboard. I can admire that. She's about the same body size and shape as me, but I'm a few inches taller. Her short stature makes her look cute, but the determined and hardened look on her face reminds me that she is fierce and not to be messed with.

"What's your name?" I asked. Something inside of me wants to know her, and I don't know why.

"Marisa," she hesitated before telling me, which laid a red flag. "What's your name?"

I dropped the red flag and assumed she was probably just nervous and shocked about my question.

"You don't need to know my name," I told her. Ethan is still in that building, and he can come out here any second now. I need to get rid of Marisa and get out of here before he spots one of us. "You need to go! Something is about to go down here, and I don't need you getting yourself involved." I'm not lying to her. Something might go down if Ethan comes out here and sees us. I just need her to leave. "Go on. Get out of here before you get in my way."

Marisa looked at me for what seemed the longest time, she still seemed confused. I'm not sure what it is about me that confuses her. She eventually turned away from me and ran back the way she came. That takes care of that, at least. Nobody else needs to get involved with this. With any luck, Ethan has gotten rid of his tail, and I can get back to tailing him myself. He'll lead me to Durin, and some answers.

I turned around to start scanning the area looking for a hiding place. Instead of spotting a hiding place, I spotted Ethan walking out of the building, and he spotted me. Our eyes locked, and it was too late for me to run or hide.

6

An Encounter

I WAS LIKE A DEER IN HEADLIGHTS, FROZEN IN PLACE, AND waiting for the speeding car to hit me. Ethan was the speeding car, but he wasn't moving toward me. He was just as frozen as I was.

"Reese?" he muttered as if his brain had only just caught up with the fact that I was standing in front of him. "Reese, what are you doing here? Do you have any idea how dangerous this is? I told you to keep your head low. It's important that you stay out of the way and wait for your memories to come back."

"Hold on a second," I interrupted him. "First, you should really try breathing in between sentences." I could have sworn his face turned red while he was raging at me. "Second, why on earth should I listen to you and anything you say? You work for Durin, and as far as I'm concerned, that makes you either my enemy or my way to get to him. Which one do you want to be?"

"Listen to me, Reese." He took a few steps toward me, and for some reason, I didn't move away. Some part of me knew him, and that part trusted him in some way. "Everything depends on you getting your memories back and staying safe until that happens. I know you don't understand any of this, but you need to trust me."

"Trust you?" The thought almost made me laugh. "Why the hell would I trust one of Durin's men?"

Ethan opened his mouth to explain further, but before he could say anything, there was a loud bang. The ground beneath us shook slightly. I threw my hands out to try and balance myself. If I didn't, I might fall over. Ethan seemed more balanced in the situation than I was. The floor stopped shaking, and when the rumbling sound faded, it was replaced by the sound of people screaming. I looked through the alleyway behind Ethan, and I managed to spot a few people running past. They were running away from something.

Ethan ran through the alleyway toward the street, and I followed after him. As we reached the street, I could see smoke in the air. I couldn't see where the smoke was coming from exactly, but it would be easy to find it if I followed the smoke. We both stood there for a few moments watching the smoke rise, and the people on the street scream and run for their lives.

Two men were running away from the smoke but not like the others. They were running toward us. They were running toward Ethan.

"Ethan! Thank God you're here," one of them yelled out.

"There was an explosion. One of Durin's rigs is under attack, and he sent us to find you. We need your help."

The men ran off, back toward the direction of the smoke. Finally, this is my chance to get to Durin. I have a feeling that he's by that rig. Why else would he send men out here looking for Ethan to come help? All I have to do now is follow them, and they will lead me straight to Durin.

Ethan moved off to follow the men, and I started to follow him. Ethan noticed me and immediately turned around to stop me.

"You have to stay out of this, Reese," he told me. He walked toward me, and I backed away from him. "I'm not sure what's going on and who is behind this attack. For now, it's too dangerous for you to get involved."

"You really think you're going to stop me?" I responded. He continued to push toward me, so I continued backing away from him. My best defense is to keep my distance. "I'm going to follow that smoke, and I'm going to that rig. If Durin is there, then nothing is going to stop me from getting to him."

Ethan moved quickly, but I can move just as fast as him. He rushed toward me. To anyone else on the street, he would be a blur in the wind. I moved away from him, becoming a blur myself. He kept pushing me back, but I had no time to look behind me. I slammed the center of my spine into a lamp pole and cried out. Ethan took advantage of the situation and moved in on me. I expected him to hit me or disable me somehow, but he went straight for my wrist.

I felt something cold against my wrist, and it quickly tightened around my skin. It pinched, but it wasn't sore. He then moved away from me. I got up and moved toward him. My intention was to launch an attack, but as I pounced on him, something grabbed hold of me and snapped me back. I looked down at my wrist.

"Shit!" I yelled out when I saw the handcuffs connecting me to the lamp pole.

I snapped my arm away from the lamp pole, this time using all of my strength, but the handcuffs didn't snap. I continued pulling on it, but it became clear that it wasn't going to break. I'm growled out of frustration. I'm stronger than this. Why can't I break a stupid pair of handcuffs off of my wrist?

I turned to look at Ethan.

"Take this off of me," I demanded.

"Sorry, but I can't let you get yourself killed. Not yet," he stood up and dusted himself off. "As I said, you're too important. You need to keep out of this until you get your head straight and your memories come back."

I hissed at him and pulled on the handcuffs again. Whatever they're made out of, it is hindering my abilities. I can't break them. They're making me weak as if I were only human.

"You can get out of those, I'm sure, but I'm hoping they'll keep you busy for long enough. At least long enough for me to sort this mess out."

With that, he ran off and left me alone by the lamp pole. As soon as he was gone, I used my free hand to pick the lock. I've been in this situation before, and I've gotten out of it too. I raised my hand in front of me and focused on the nail of my index finger. This was a skill that took me weeks to perfect. The nail began to grow. It turned black at the root, and the color spread to the sharp, pointed tip as the nail grew long like a small, thin dagger. Doing this was easy enough. I can usually make all of my nails grow longer and sharper than this in seconds. Still, with the handcuffs dampening my power, it took everything I had and all my concentration to make just one nail grow. I think the only reason it worked was that the handcuffs aren't on both my wrists. I would be completely powerless if they were.

I started picking the lock on the handcuffs. Ethan was right, this would keep me busy for a while, but once I get out of it, I'll still be able to follow the pillar of smoke in the air.

"I didn't know you were a skilled lockpicker."

I heard the voice, and I recognized it, but it took me a few seconds before I realized that it wasn't in my head. I looked up from the handcuffs to see Marisa standing over me, and she wasn't alone.

She stood there, towering over me, surrounded by police officers. They all had their guns trained on me as if I was still a threat while handcuffed to a lamp pole. I scanned the rest of the street to see that it was empty, aside from me, Marisa, and the police officers. They had blocked the street off on both sides with police cars, and the only thought that came to my mind was how I didn't notice them. I was so fixated on freeing myself and chasing down Ethan that I allowed myself to be surrounded by the police force. Not that I would have been able to escape.

I looked back at Marisa, making sure she could see the rage in my eyes. I was stupid to trust her.

"I'm guessing everything you told me is a lie," I mumbled.

"Not everything," she replied with a slight smile pulling at the corner of her lips. "My name really is Marisa. Detective Marisa Morgan at your service." She faked a curtsey. "I've been looking for you for a long time, and here you are all tied up for me, and the only thing missing a big pretty bow to top off my present."

I scowled at her, "Stop toying with me and get this over with will you."

"As you wish," she turned to face the officers. "Let's bring her in boys. Those handcuffs are the same as the ones we use. We should be able to use one of our keys to get her unattached from the lamp pole. Make sure you keep the one side on her wrist, so they continue to work the way they're supposed to."

She turned to smile at me while one of the officers moved forward to carry out her orders. There was something so smug about her smile. I wanted to punch her. Somehow it also made me like her more. I can't deny this is something I would do.

The man used a set of keys from his pocket to unlock the handcuff connected to the lamp pole. Another officer then lifted me off the ground. At the same time, he pulled both my arms behind my back and attached the handcuff to my other wrist. I don't know what these handcuffs are made of, but they've taken away all of my power. I'm just a human.

I didn't fight them as they escorted me to one of their patrol cars. There was no point in fighting them now. They had guns, and I was outnumbered. If it weren't for these handcuffs, then none of that would matter, but for now, I'm at their mercy, and I have to bide my time until I can free myself and get my power back.

Marisa climbed into the passenger seat in front of me and told the officer to drive. I eyed her from my cage in the back. I want to be angry. I want to bare my teeth and snap at her, but something won't let me. Some part of me likes her in some way, I won't deny that. She intrigues me and inspires my curiosity. No human has been able to lie to me and get away with it. That is impressive.

"That cute little story you spun about your sister must have been a lie then, huh?" I asked her. It was a long drive to the nearest police station. I might as well have some fun along the way. "I have to admit I've never been successfully lied to. I'm a bit upset about it."

"You'll get over it," she replied. "I'm sure you've done your fair share of lying in your lifetime. For the sake of your sanity, let's call it karma, shall we." I spotted a slight smile pull at the corner of her mouth. She was pleased with herself. "I would save my breath if I were you."

"Why, will I need it any more than usual?" I leaned forward until my face was pressed against the bars separating me from them. "You'd be surprised by how long I can go without breathing."

"I know all about demons and their little tricks," she turned to face me, and our faces were so close I could have bitten her if it weren't for the bars. "You should save your boasting for the captain."

"The captain!" I sat back in my car. "Now, what does the captain of the police want with little old me?"

She leaned in closer until her forehead was pressed against the bars, and she smiled an especially devilish smile at me.

She licked her lips, then whispered, "Spoilers."

7

A Deal to Be Made

THE POLICE CAR STOPPED OUTSIDE THE POLICE STATION, and Marisa pulled me out of the back. She led me inside while two officers walked beside me, holding my arms. As if they actually needed to do that. With these cuffs on, I'm useless. I need to know what they're made of and how they work. They must be magic or something if they are capable of basically rendering me human while I'm wearing them.

As we walked through the station, I drew the eyes of almost everyone I walked past. It was as if they were waiting for me. Marisa took me straight to the back of the building. She's probably going to put me in a cage and leave me there. That would be a mistake. When I'm put in a cage, it's more likely I'm going to act like a wild animal. I hate being trapped.

We stopped in front of a frosted glass door that had the words Captain Reeds written in small gold letters across the top. Marisa opened the door and told the officers to sit me down. They dumped me on one of the chairs and left.

I looked back to see Marisa leaning against the door and smiling down at me.

"Now don't you go anywhere," she giggled. "I'll be right back."

She pulled the door closed, and I heard a click as she locked it. As soon as her footsteps faded down the hallway, I began my escape attempt. I grunted and growled as I pulled my wrists apart. I stretched the chain of the hand-cuff, hoping it would snap and free my hands. I used all of the strength that I could manage, but it appeared that I have little to no strength at all.

I leaned forward and bit down on the chain with my teeth. I bit down hard, and my jaw snapped back open the moment my teeth collided against the metal. The force of the collision vibrated through my mouth and brought tears to my eyes. No matter how painful it was, I needed to keep trying. I stood up and bent over, placing the chain of the handcuffs underneath my one shoe. I stepped down on it hard and pulled my arms up. Sweat droplets formed on my forehead, and I felt the cold, wetness drip down my face. I have never sweated like this in my life. I've never exerted myself to this point. For as long as I can remember, which isn't long at all, nothing has ever made me work so hard before.

I collapsed back into the chair as I found myself out of breath. I can hear my heart pounding in my ears as I breathe in deeply and rapidly to get some oxygen flowing back to my brain. I need to know what these are made of. Next time I see Ethan, I'll ask him right before I punch him in the face for putting me in this situation. As much as I didn't want to admit it, I'm trapped like a caged animal.

Escaping wasn't an option, and sitting down like this is boring. I stood up and walked to the door. I tried it, just in case, but it was definitely locked. I walked around the rest of the room and tested the comfort level of the furniture. The chair I was in was more comfortable than the couch, but I could lie down on the couch, which gives it bonus points. The chair behind the desk in the middle of the room must be the captain's chair. Obviously, this is the most comfortable furniture in the room, and it's a swivel chair, which gives it extra bonus points.

I sat in the chair and used my feet to make it spin. The room blurred past me as it spun faster and faster. While spinning, I noticed something hanging on the wall behind the desk. It was so blurred that I couldn't see much, but I noticed one name written in big red letters right in the middle of it. I stomped my feet down on the floor and stopped the chair instantly.

I got up and walked toward the investigation board sitting in the corner of the room. I wondered how I hadn't noticed it sooner. Durin's name is written directly in the middle of the board in large, red letters. Black lines are leading from his name to other points on the board. These points appear to be the names of men, places, and incidents they are investigating. A few pictures are hanging on the board, some of them are of men working under Durin, and some are of places they suspect to be one of his hideouts or places of operation. I read through it as fast as I could. Marisa could be back at any moment, and I don't want to be interrupted before I'm ready.

I didn't recognize any of the names except for two, Ethan's and my own. For some reason, I'm on the board with a big, red question mark next to my picture. Next to Ethan's name, they have written "right-hand man" in red. I had a feeling Ethan was high up in the ranks, but I had no idea he could be Durin's, right-hand man.

It's clear to me that they've been investigating Durin for a long time, much longer than me. An idea popped into my head. I put the idea to bed for now until I can find out more about why I'm here. I was only halfway through all the information on the board, but I had no choice but to leave it for now. I ran back to my chair and sat down. I swung my one leg over the other and leaned back into the chair to appear casual.

I heard the click as the door unlocked, and two people entered the room. I didn't turn around to look at them because I wanted to seem uninterested. I watched from the corner of my eye as Marisa closed the door. An old man, maybe around 60 years old, wearing a polished uniform, walked around the desk and sat down in the swivel chair. Marisa walked behind the desk and stood beside him. They both looked down at me, and for a moment, I felt like a little girl who'd just been sent to the principal's office for skipping class.

"So, this is the great vigilante I've heard about," the man who I assume is Captain Reeds stated. "Reese, isn't it?"

"Only my friends get to call me that," I replied in an uninterested tone. "You can refer to me as Vigilante for now."

"I'm not the one that wants to be your friend," he explained. "Detective Morgan here insisted on bringing you in. She has a few plans for you. At the moment, I'm not in a position to look a gift horse in the mouth."

"The last people who didn't look their gift horse in the mouth were invaded, so I strongly suggest you rethink that statement."

"Reese," Marisa stepped forward, "I believe we both have something to gain from working together."

I uncrossed my legs and then crossed them the opposite way because they were getting uncomfortable. It also made me look more in control of the situation than I actually was. The more casual I can look, the better.

"Go on," I hummed, "I'm listening."

"You and the police in this city both want the same thing, Durin's demise," she explained. "You showed up out of nowhere about seven months ago, and you've been tearing down Durin's operations one by one. We've been watching you for the past five months. So far, you've only attacked his small operations, but you've been working your way up the ranks. This was when I got the idea that you were trying to find a way to Durin." She walked to the front of the desk and sat down on it in front of me. "We both want to bring him down."

"That's a nice story, but what's your point?"

Captain Reeds stood up and walked over to the investigation board. He pulled it out from the corner and pushed it to the middle of the room. Then he stood beside it and looked straight at me with emotionless eyes.

"Let's get one thing straight here," he huffed through his mustache-covered lips. "I don't trust you. You're a loose cannon, and if it were up to me, you'd be kept in those handcuffs for the rest of your days or transferred to the Silver Bars Prison until we find a use for you. However, Marisa is one of my best detectives, and she believes we can use your help to catch Durin."

"You want me to work with you to bring down Durin?" I was talking to myself, but they both nodded as if I was asking them the question. "Why?"

"We've both been working toward the same goal," Marisa explained further. She got up and walked over to the investigation board. "You've been picking apart Durin's operation one rig at a time, and so have we." She pointed to spots on the board where several of Durin's small rigs were crossed out with a red marker. "Some of these operations you took down and some of them we took down, but all of them are small and meaningless compared to the big picture. I believed that if we worked together, we could maximize our efforts and go for the big picture, which is Durin himself."

"I get what you're trying to say here," I said as I stood and walked toward the board, "but what makes you think we'll be any more effective working together than we are working alone?"

Marisa smiled and leaned against the board. She likes leaning against things when she's feeling confident about herself.

"The reason you haven't been successful at getting to Durin is that you lack my skills. I'm an excellent investigator. As Captain Reeds said, I'm the best detective in the city. I was good enough to catch you after all. Vice-versa, the only reason I haven't had any success is that I lack your skills, those skills being pure, unkempt demon rage, and strength. Almost all of Durin's men are demons, which can make it difficult for us weak humans to compete with. I think we'd make a good team."

I looked at the investigation board for a while then looked back at Marisa. The offer is clearly a good one, but there has to be a catch somewhere. I want to get to Durin more than anything, and so do they. She's right that if we work together, we will stand a better chance. I'm not one to go around trusting people I don't know.

"Why now?" I asked her. "I've been after Durin for months, but from the look of this board, you've been after him for years. Why do you have the sudden urge to end his operations now?"

"We've received some new information that has changed the game a bit," Captain Reeds answered my question, so I spun round to face him. "This city is filled with different gangs, and Durin's is just one of them. Some of our undercover men had received information that one of the big chiefs is building a weapon of some kind. This weapon could have devastating effects on the city, and we have reason to believe that Durin is the one building it."

"Devastating how?" I attempted to cross my arms, but the handcuffs made that impossible, so I just stood there with my hands dangling in front of me.

"If our information is correct," Marisa responded. Hence, I spun around to look at her, "this weapon will have enough power to level half the city."

"Why the hell would someone want to do that?"

"We don't know, and we don't care," Captain Reeds replied, and I didn't bother turning to look at him this time.

"Our job is to stop them, and that's all we need to know," Marisa continued. She rifled through her pockets and pulled out a set of keys. "Are you with us?" She asked as she unlocked my handcuffs and pulled them off my wrists.

The feeling was instantaneous as my strength and power returned to my body. The warmth rushed through my body and made my blood boil. I couldn't help but let my ability show a little as it was released. My eyes felt hot as their color changed to a pitch black. A bright sheen rolled over them, and my normal purple color returned to my eyes. I pulled my power back inside me and let it move through my body a little while longer before locking it back up. I could feel it was still there, but I hid it until I needed it again. I looked straight at Marisa and gave her a toothy grin.

"Before I agree," I told her, "I want to talk to you privately."

Marisa looked me up and down then nodded her head

in agreement. She kept the same smug smile on her face the whole time. Captain Reeds walked with us to a nearby interrogation room, then closed the door and locked us in. We were alone in the room with just a metal table and two metal chairs, both bolted to the floor.

She walked to the other end of the table and looked at me. I stared straight back at her, and we began to circle the table. With each step I took, she took one too. I eyed her, and she studied me as the only thing keeping us apart was the metal table. If only she knew I could vault the table and slam her up against the wall within a second. She wouldn't even see me until my face was an inch away from hers, and my hand was around her neck. I wasn't going to do that, but I loved thinking about the fact that I could do it. It was nice to be free again.

"What is it you want to discuss?" Marisa broke the silence by asking me that. "We can't circle the table all day long unless you were planning on playing a game of musical chairs."

I smiled and held back a laugh. She made me smile more than I have in the months since I left the hospital. I would be lying if I said I didn't like it.

"You said you've been watching me for the past five months," she nodded in response. "Then you know how I work. You know what happens to people who get in my way."

"I understand the way you operate and trust me, I have no intention of getting in your way." She stopped circling and crossed her arms, pushing her one hip out to the side. "We share the same goal, it's only logical we help each other reach that goal. I can agree to let you do your thing, as long as you work with me and let me do my thing."

I mimicked her crossed arms and popped hip and grinned at her.

"Okay then, we have a deal," she reached her hand out to me, and I eyed it. "If we get into any battles, you need to stay out of it. I can't fight and protect you at the same time. If you get hurt, I won't take any responsibility."

"Don't worry," she said, keeping her hand held out, "I know how to handle myself."

I waited for a moment, but I couldn't see any reason not to join them. This was the best break I've gotten in a while. Durin is looking closer than ever now. I reached my hand out to meet hers. We shook and sealed the deal. I'm now partnered with the best detective in the city.

"Do I get a badge now?" I asked her. "If I do, I want it to say Detective Demon."

8

Cold Case

I LEAPED FROM BUILDING TO BUILDING, SLIDING DOWN PIPES and running across rooftops, following the smoke pillar in the air. After wearing those handcuffs, I felt freer now than I ever did before. I let all my power out. I ran faster, jumped higher, landed harder, and I enjoyed every second of it.

The sirens blared in my ears as Marisa drove beside me in her car. She did her best to follow my moves and keep up with me, but cars are much slower than demons. I had to slow down, so she didn't lose me. I didn't mind. The smoke got thicker, which meant we were getting closer. I could only hope that Ethan or Durin was still there, and I haven't missed any action.

I can see the wreckage ahead of me. It looks like someone blew up a cargo ship. It's half sunk, and the smoke trail is rising from its engine room. I dropped down from the last building on the way there and ran along the ground. I moved fast but not too fast to see. Marisa's car drove up behind me and followed me into the shipping yard. She had to turn to follow the road to the ship, but I sprinted straight through the shipping containers and made a beeline for the ship.

I reached it first and used my senses to scan the ship. I took a deep breath and breathe in the scent of the area through my nose. I let everything in. I let in all the scents in the area, the smell of the salty seawater, the sting of the smoke, the stink of the raw fish, and blood. The ship reeked of blood and smoke. It was strong but not strong enough. Any blood that is on the vessel is dried up and old. I sniffed the air one more time, but I didn't pick up any more scents.

Marisa turned off the sirens on her car as she pulled up beside me and parked. She got out and gasped at the sight of the destroyed ship. She walked up to me just as I muttered underneath my breath.

"Shit!"

"What is it," she asked in response to my reaction. "What's wrong?"

"We're too late," I responded while baring my teeth. "Whatever happened here, it's over, and we missed it."

"Are you sure? We should search the ship to make certain. I'll call it in."

She walked to the driver's side of her car and pulled out her radio, but I interrupted her before she could use it.

"There's no point! Whoever was on the ship is either dead or injured and long gone. The only thing I can smell is smoke and blood, but it's old blood. That means whoever the blood belongs to is dead, or they left a pool of blood behind as they left the scene. There's no fresh blood here."

Marisa stared at me for a moment as she put her radio back down.

"I'm guessing fresh blood would mean someone's still alive?" She asked me, and I admired the fact that she was paying attention or trying to. I nodded in response. "Okay, so what do we do now?"

I shrugged my shoulders, "Isn't this the part where you start using those 'investigative skills' of yours?" I used my fingers to mimic quotation marks when I said investigation skills. I could tell by her scowl that she didn't like that.

She slammed the driver's door closed and moved to the trunk of the car. She opened it up and started shuffling through something. I walked to the back of the vehicle to see what she was doing. There were multiple piles of papers, notebooks, and files in the trunk, and she was searching through them to find the right one. She pulled one out and flipped through the pages casually while I looked over her shoulder.

I let a smile spread across my face as I glanced at her face and then back to the folder in her hands. I like that I'm taller than her. It made glancing over her shoulder easier, and it made it easy for me to look down at her face. She was concentrating hard now. She bit down on her lower lip and narrowed her eyes when she concentrated. It was cute.

"According to this file, this was one of Durin's shipments," Marisa finally started after she finished flipping through the file. "We've known about it for months and been waiting for it to arrive. It was sent here all the way from Africa."

"How does this help us?" I asked her, still glancing over her shoulder.

"Well, we have to think about it for a moment," she turned around and sat down on the open trunk's lip. "Durin is one of the biggest gang leaders in the city, the others are big too, but none of them as big as him. We have to ask ourselves, who would attack one of Durin's shipments if none of the gangs in the city want to touch him with a ten-foot pole."

I sat down next to her and leaned back against her car. She crossed her arms and looked at me, so I did the same.

"I'm guessing you already know the answer to that question."

She smiled, and I could tell she was pleased with herself once again.

"As a matter of fact, I do," she stood up again and started searching through the files and folders in the trunk again. "He's a fairly new part of the puzzle. We're not sure when he arrived in the city, but he's been making a mess for about five months. No one has seen him, the only people we see are his henchmen and it seems that ever since he arrived, he's been targeting other gangs in the city. He tore down a smaller gang that we've been going after, and he left nothing behind. He's had his eyes on Durin's operation for at least a week now. His henchmen have attacked three separate shipments of his."

"Whoever this guy is, he has a beef with Durin just like us," I added, trying to take everything she told me and scale it down.

"I think it's more than that," she added as she pulled out the file she was looking for. She held the file close to her chest and looked at me. "I said we're not sure when this guy arrived in the city, but I have my suspicions. I believe he showed up at least ten months ago and has been lying low up until now. I believe that guy has something to do with you, Reese."

I narrowed my eyes and raised my eyebrows at her. She handed me the file she'd been holding. I opened it up and read it. It detailed an assault that happened around seven months ago. A young girl was beaten to near death, but she disappeared from the scene before emergency services could arrive. When emergency services did come, instead of finding a young girl, they found three demons, dead and drained of their blood. I turned the page. The only evidence found was security footage that showed the three demons sacrificing themselves to save the young girl. Then she got up and stumbled out of view of the camera. The end of the file states that the young girl is a Jane Doe and still missing.

I closed the folder and handed it back to her.

"What does that have to do with anything?" I asked her.

She sat back down but at an angle so she could face me this time.

"I've been working on this case ever since it showed up, and Reese, I'm convinced that this young woman is you."

I gasped and pushed away from the car, "That can't be. The file said the women disappeared before emergency services arrived. I woke up in the hospital, so how can that be so."

She pulled two more files out of the trunk and did her best to explain them to me.

"This file is of a report of a young woman found wandering the streets, barefoot, covered in blood, and dazed. She was picked up and taken to the nearest hospital. She was a Jane Doe, and as far as the doctors could tell, the blood was hers, but there were no injuries on her body. This woman was found only one block away from where the other young woman was attacked and on the same night, only an hour later." She put the file down and looked straight at me. "I always believed they were the same woman, but since the one was beaten to within an inch of her life, and the other had no injuries on her, no one else shared my beliefs."

I took a few deep breaths to calm myself, and I sat back

down beside her. I was silent for a few moments, and she left me to think about it. She stayed quiet while the information sank in. I silently thanked her for that.

"Okay," I finally spoke. "Let's say the women in these two files are me. What does that have to do with any of this? How can it help us catch Durin and find the other new bad guy?"

Marisa smiled as if she was proud of me and somewhat proud of herself. She opened up the last of the three files she was holding and read it to me.

"This file comes from the same night," she explained. "Around the same time, the young woman, or you, were beaten to within an inch of your life there was a secret war going on. Hundreds of Durin's men were found dead all over the city along with the dead bodies of henchmen from another gang. At the time, we thought it was a random skirmish between gangs, but we didn't recognize the men from the other gang. The only men we recognized were Durin's." She took a deep breath and threw the file back in the trunk. "Now I believe that those men belonged to this new guy and that he took his first move that night. He tried to tear Durin's system apart, but he failed and went back to hiding. Reese, you were beaten and nearly killed that night, but three demons sacrificed themselves to save you."

"I was part of the war," I breathed as I realized the picture Marisa was trying to paint for me. "I was fighting in the war, which means I must have been fighting for one of them."

"Yes!" Marisa cried out as if I'd just won a prize. "We just don't know what side you were on. We know that what happened that night made you lose your memories."

"Except for one thing," I added. "I always remembered Durin, and I always wanted to take him down."

"Good, so I think that if we follow the breadcrumbs

from that night, we could find out who you were before you lost your memories."

I stood up, and Marisa stood up with me. I stepped away from the car, and she closed the trunk.

"Reese, we can find out who you were before. We could figure out what you nearly died for, and that could lead us to Durin. You were in that fight for a reason. This is your origin story! Isn't it exciting?"

My face was twisted in anger, and I scowled. I thought about it, but I didn't want to believe it. If I was part of that fight, I was working for one of these gang leaders. I knew it couldn't have been Durin, and I wasn't willing to believe I was working for this other guy either. I'm not a bad person. Marisa should have kept her nose out of it. She's snatching at straws that don't exist, and if that's what it takes to be the best detective in the city, then I have less faith in her skills now than I did before.

"Reese, what's wrong?" she asked me, obviously noticing the foul expression on my face.

"What gives you the right to meddle in my life and tell me who I am?" I growled at her. "I don't know who that woman is and what happened to her is sad, but she is not me. I would never work for one of these gangs. I've been spending the past seven months of my life tearing them down and tracking down Durin. Now you want to tell me that I might have worked for one of them. What the hell gives you the right to do that?"

Marisa put her hands out in front of her as a gesture to calm me down, and she backed away from me.

"That's not what I meant by it," she explained in a calm and soft voice. She sounded like she wanted to be my friend, but I felt like ripping her apart. "I know you're nothing like the woman you were back then. You've lost your memories, and you're a completely different person now, I get that. I only meant to help you. You need closure, Reese, and we need to catch Durin. The only way to do both those things is to find out what happened that night and find out who you were." She leaned against the car. "Tell me I'm wrong, and I'll drop it."

I growled under my breath, and my eyes flashed black for a second. She's obviously right, but I wasn't about to tell her that. Everything Marisa said had woken something up inside of me. Memories I didn't know I had. I shook my head to clear it and stepped away from her.

"I think we should go our separate ways," I muttered. "I don't need you to find Durin, I've got a lead, and I'm going to chase him down." I turned to walk away, but she grabbed my arm and turned me back to face her.

"Reese," she yelled at me. I could see she was more upset and hurt than angry. "Don't be stupid. The captain trusted you and went out on a limb to bring you in on this operation. You can't go running around half-cocked and mess it up for all of us."

I smiled the smug smile she usually shows me and pulled away from her. Before she could stop me, I leaped up onto the nearest building and ran away. She would never be able to find me. I'm too fast for her and her car. I came to terms with the fact that this might be the last time I would ever see Detective Marisa Morgan.

9

Ambushed!

I RAN FOR A WHILE. I'M NOT SURE WHERE I WAS RUNNING to, but I knew I needed to get away from Marisa, as far away as possible. I made my way to the other side of the city before I felt too tired to run anymore. I used my full strength the whole time, so I could move as fast as possible. That tired me out quickly. I found a nice high roof and took some time to rest on it.

I sat on the edge of the roof and looked down. This was one of the tallest buildings in the city, and it gave me a beautiful view. I looked down and watched the people carry on with their lives. They walked around and drove their cars. They're all blind to the chaos going on around them. Most of them probably don't even know about the existence of demons. I was surprised to find out that Marisa knew about demons. It seemed unfair to me that the humans got to go on with their lives like nothing else is going on around them, and I have to see the world for what it really is.

The longer I sat in silence, the stronger my memories of that night became. Marisa was right about one thing. I was that girl who got beaten to within an inch of her life seven months ago. I didn't want to admit it, but the memories are there. They were hidden just below the surface, but today Marisa broke them free.

Images of three men kneeling over me flashed past my eyes. I saw blood, demon blood, lots of it. It poured over me, black as oil, thick and hot. I didn't just see it pouring over me; I could feel it flowing into me. It burned every inch of my body and boiled inside of me. I became hot and uncomfortable, but I kept going. I needed to dig deeper into my memories if I hoped to get any answers.

The three men collapsed on the floor beside me. Another image flashed past my eyes. I struggled to my feet and looked down at my hands. They were covered in blood, but it wasn't demon blood. It was red and warm, human blood. The three male bodies formed a circle on the floor behind me. I stepped out of the circle and stumbled into the dark. I dug for more, but all I could see was darkness, all I could feel was the cold of the night. There was no more for me to see.

I couldn't believe that was all there was to see. That was the only memory I have of my past life. I couldn't believe it took Marisa to unlock them. I felt empty inside as if something had been taken from me. I didn't have an identity to start with, but I felt like it had been stripped away from me, and now I am no one. I'm just another unsolved case file in the trunk of a detective's car. I'm just another Jane Doe that nobody cared about.

Marisa cared about me. I needed to remind myself of that. She had all those case files in her trunk, which meant that she cared about them in some way. She cared enough to work on it even though it had gone cold. She cared enough to see all the connections, even though everyone else told her that there were no connections. Marisa did care about me, which means I'm not just another Jane Doe.

I can't think about that now, though. I have a lead that will take me to Durin, and I need to follow it. I'm sure Marisa will find me again at some point. She is the best detective in the city, after all.

I stood up on the edge and focused my power toward my senses. I pulled all of the power from other parts of my body, then I breathed in deeply through my nose. My sense of smell is good, but if I'm to find one scent in this whole city, then I need to focus all of my power and energy to that ability. I scanned through all the scents in the city. The smell of fresh, warm hotdogs with mustard and ketchup was strong, and it made my stomach growl. I snapped my concentration away from it and focused harder. I know what scent I'm looking for, but I have to find it and set it apart from all the other scents.

There it is. I isolated the smell of blood that matched the blood I smelt on the ship. It was dry and old at the time, but I knew it belonged to someone who had escaped the attack. I found him. From his scent, I can tell that he's close and he's still injured. He's a demon, but I figured he hasn't had enough time to stop and heal himself. I hoped he was enough of a lead to help me find Durin.

I made my way down to the ground and walked among the crowd toward the scent. I needed to get close to this man, so I needed to act as human as possible. If he didn't see me as a threat, he wouldn't treat me as one, not until it's too late. The scent led me away from the crowd and down a series of alleyways. That didn't bother me. I live in alleys, and I feel most comfortable in them. I climbed up to the top of a building and leaped to the next rooftop to take a shortcut. I was getting close now. I dropped back down into the alleyway and sniffed the air. He was only a few feet away from me now. When I sniffed the air, I smelt something else, something that shouldn't be there.

I smelt the blood of others. It was fresh, and they were all around me. I had only a second to react as they jumped out of the shadows and down from roofs to surround me. It's a trap. I leaped into the air and took a defensive possession at the end of the alleyway. There was a wall to my back, but at least that meant no one could tackle me from behind. This was the best position I could take. They had to come to me, and I could see all of them at all times.

I'm not sure who these men are, but I suspect that they are Durin's. I don't know how they knew I would be here or set up a trap for me. Unless I walked into a trap set for someone else. All these questions can be answered once I render most of them unconscious and leave one of them alive enough to answer them.

The first man moved toward me. He was a demon, so he blurred past the space between us and attempted to grab my neck. Ethan was the first demon I met to match my speed, so this man wasn't fast enough. I saw him coming and grabbed his arm before he could wrap his fingers around my neck.

I squeezed around his arm and allowed my nails to grow into his flesh. He cried out as I drew blood, and it dripped down his arm. I twisted his arm behind his back, making him spin around. I was so fast and strong that I turned his arm too far back and snapped his shoulder out of its socket. The popping sound it made echoed through the alleyway followed by his high-pitched scream. I was sure he was dealt with now, so I pushed him away. He stumbled forward and collapsed on the floor face first.

I turned my attention to the other men, but they seemed hesitant now. I took a step forward, and they stepped back. I smiled. Before they could make another move, I leaped up onto the alleyway wall. I ran across the wall and blurred past them. They could barely keep track of my movements, but they managed to see me duck into an adjoining alleyway. They followed after me as fast as they could. I ran. I wasn't sure where I was running to, but I knew I needed to get away from them. I could take them all on one by one, but I was worried they wouldn't come at me one by one. I needed to separate them to avoid the probability of that happening.

I ran out into an open space between two buildings but away from the public street. There was no need to get any humans involved in this fight. I could hear their footsteps close behind me. This isn't a good place to fight, so I need to get out of here. I jumped up and landed on the rooftop. I made sure it was a loud landing so they would follow me up here. I glanced over my shoulder to see the five of them leaping onto the roof behind me. At least now I know that they're all demons.

I ran as fast as I could, but two of them were gaining on me. They must be the fastest of the group. I didn't want to find out if they were the strongest too. I scanned the area for a suitable place to continue my fight with them. I needed a place not too wide open, with multiple exits, and not too narrow. While scanning for the area, I spotted something I didn't think I would. I saw Marisa's police car, with Marisa standing next to it.

I dropped down from the rooftops and ran toward her car. She saw me and smiled, then she saw the men running after me and scowled. I jumped onto the hood of her car and slid across to the other side while she pulled her gun out from its holster and started firing at them. Those bullets wouldn't do anything to a demon, but they took cover anyway. I crouched behind the car.

"How did you find me?" I yelled at her so she could hear me over the gunshots.

She emptied her clip then ducked down behind the car with me.

"You'd be surprised how noticeable a woman leaping from rooftop to rooftop through the center of the city is," she replied. At the same time, she searched through the bag beside her for another clip. "We were getting calls in from all over the place, and they all led me to this area."

"Well, I won't say thanks for coming, but I will say thanks for shooting them." I glanced over the hood of the car. The men were regaining their composure and getting ready to pursue me again.

"Are they demons or humans?" Marisa asked me as she clipped a new magazine into her gun.

"Demons, definitely demons."

She grabbed the big bag sitting between us and pulled it open. She dug inside of it while I watched the men walk closer. She pulled out a thick piece of rolled-up leather that was tied together with a black ribbon. She unties the ribbon and unrolls the piece of leather out on the floor in front of her. Inside the folded leather is some strange equipment and weapons of some kind. She picked up one that looked like a big revolver with an old wooden handle.

"What the hell is that?" I asked her as I watched her load it with bullets twice the size of any regular bullet I've seen.

"These weapons are designed to kill a demon," she replied. "The bullets are made of pure silver mixed with a bit of magnetite. The gun is big, which makes it more powerful when it shoots the bullet. In other words, it makes a hole too big for the demon to heal, and the silver and magnetite react with the demon's blood, negating its healing ability."

"Great, thanks for the science lesson, but can you actually fire that thing at one of the demons walking toward us with the intent to kill us?"

As I said it, Marisa cocked the gun and jumped back up. She aimed the gun at the closest demon and pulled the trigger. I watched as a hole bigger than my fist burst through the chest of one of the men. Black blood splattered all over the pavement by his feet. Some of it even splattered on the men near him. They jumped away from him, and some of them spat the blood out of their mouths. My eyes widened, and I couldn't help but smile.

I looked back down at the rest of the strange equipment. Some of them looked like guns, one looked like a grenade, but most of them looked like different kinds of knives.

"I assume the rest of those things are also designed to kill demons," I said. At the same time, Marisa loaded another bullet into her big gun.

"Yep! Take one and have a go if you want."

I grabbed what looked like a long, thin, dagger with a silver hilt decorated with a purple jewels line. I held it tight in my grip and darted around the front of the car. Marisa took a shot at one of the men while I ran at another. I had the knife at the ready as I leaped at him.

I sliced the knife at his chest. He attempted to block it with his arms, but where a typical knife would have bounced off his skin, this knife sliced almost straight through. He cried out and lashed his legs out at me. I dodged his kicks and darted back into his body with the knife in front of me. The knife sliced into his ribs easily. He doubled over and fell to the ground as I pulled the knife free from his body. I had blood on my wrist, but I could clean it off once I've finished with the other men.

I turned to face the last man remaining, and I assumed

Marisa dealt with the other two. I moved toward him, knife at the ready once again, but I stopped when I heard a scream followed by a loud bang. My head whipped around in the direction of the sound. The next thing I saw was Marisa lying on the ground, her chest drenched in blood, pointing her gun up at the demon standing over her. The demon had a large hole in his stomach, and soon he wasn't standing anymore. I looked back at the last demon remaining. He glanced back and forth between Marisa and me.

I took a step toward him, and he threw his hands up to stop me.

"Wait, Reese!" He yelled out, and I stopped in my tracks. "None of this was supposed to happen. We were just supposed to give you a message. Durin says he wants you back on the mission. Meet us at the old swing."

The demon looked back at Marisa again and then at me one more time. He turned and leaped up onto the rooftop. I wanted to follow him, but I couldn't. Instead, I ran to see how badly Marisa was injured. She was still lying on the ground in front of the car with the demon's dead body beside her. I kicked him aside and knelt down.

She's pressing her hand tightly against a spot below her ribs and just above her hip. Blood is squeezing out between her fingers and around the edges of her hand. She tried to sit up but winced at the pain and lay back down.

"Is it bad?" I asked her since I have no idea what to do in this situation.

"I'm fine," she coughed and gasped as she tried to move again. "What the hell was that guy talking about? What's the old swing?"

"I don't know, and I don't need to know." I stood up and stared at the rooftop the man had leaped up to. I still have his scent, so if I left, now I can follow him. I need some proper answers. I can't just stay here. "I need to follow that guy. He's our only lead to Durin right now."

"No," Marisa gasped as she tried to move again. "Backup is on the way. Once they get here, we can get the scene under control, get my wound checked, and go after him."

"There's no time for that," I hissed at her. "I have his scent now. If I don't follow him, I'll lose the scent, and we'll lose him."

"You can't keep going off on your own, Reese!" she yelled at me and coughed. "We're partners! We shook on it, remember. Partners don't just run off while their partner is bleeding on the ground."

"I have to go, Marisa," I walked away from her. "I'm sorry."

10

Unexpected Guests

I DIDN'T WANT TO TELL MARISA, BUT I'M STARTING TO think that she's right about me being connected to Durin. I was part of the war that night. I was beaten to within an inch of my life and rescued by demons. All of that seems to tie me to Durin in some way. Now, more than ever, I need to find some proper answers about who I was before that night.

I didn't need to leap up onto the roof. I have his scent, so all I need to do is follow it. I ran through the alleyways. I kept the knife in my hand. It might come in useful if I encounter another group of demons.

While I tracked down the scent, I thought about how much Marisa knew about demons. She seemed to know a lot more than I do, and she's only a human. I know what demons can do only from the experience of doing those things myself, but this was the first time I knew that there was a more efficient way to kill them.

I'm getting close to the scent, but at this point, I'm not sure which part of the city I'm in. All I see are dark alley-ways leading to busy streets and roads. I climb up the nearest building side so I can get a better sense of where I am. I want a better view of the city, but I don't want to draw attention to myself. As I get to the top of the building, I realize that someone is waiting for me.

"What are you doing?" Ethan asks me while I tumble onto the rooftop.

"Sorry, I didn't realize this viewpoint was taken," I responded. "I'll go find another rooftop to stand on."

"Cut it out, Reese," he snapped at me and blurred toward me. I stood still as he circled me. "You're different, and it's not just because you've lost your memories." He leaned in close to the back of my neck and sniffed me. "You smell different than I remember. You act differently and talk differently." He stepped in front of me and reached his hand out to my face. "You're not the Reese I used to know."

He touched my cheek with his fingertips, and every instinct I had, told me to pull away from him. I didn't pull away. This felt familiar in some way. It felt right. It felt safe. I had been in this position before, with his hand pressed against my face and his eyes staring into mine. It all felt so familiar. He lifted his other hand and pressed it to my other cheek as he moved closer. I was hypnotized. I couldn't move even if I wanted to, and some small part of me did want to break free of this spell.

Something woke me up, I'm not sure what, but I came to my senses and pulled away from him.

"I need to get to Durin," I told him.

He nodded his head, "I agree, but now isn't the right time. Durin will call you in when he is ready for you."

"So it's true then," I sighed and cursed under my breath. My hands clenched into fists, and my insides burned. "I work for Durin, or at least I used to. How can that be true if I hate him so much? All I've wanted, for as long as I can remember, is to kill Durin. Why? What the hell is Durin even doing, and how could I be involved?"

Ethan stared at me, blankly as if I'd just hit him in the face with a brick. I was a mystery to him that was certain.

"What is going on?" He raised his voice. "Reese, you need to understand something…"

He walked toward me as he spoke, and I prepared myself to finally hear some answers. Before Ethan could say anything of use to me, footsteps echoed below us, and he sniffed the air. He growled at the scent, and his head snapped toward me.

"Someone's coming," he whispered. "Get out of here."

He leaped to the next roof and then dropped down to the street below. When he left, the footsteps below seemed to follow after him. I am left alone once again and without answers.

THE TIME FLEW BY, and I spent the rest of the night searching for Durin. I used every skill I have learned to investigate and track down his closest contacts. The usual meeting spots were empty. It seems as if Durin is cleaning up. He knows someone is looking to get close to him, and he's keeping his cards close to his chest. No matter what I tried, I came up empty.

By the time the sun rose, it was time for me to give up and go home. I'm not one to quit, but the light from the sun and the hustle and bustle of the early morning city people made it difficult for me to do my job.

My home isn't much, but it's a roof over my head and a place I can feel safe enough to sleep. It's a small apartment in the center of the city. The center is the best because it gives me quick access to any part of the city. It's on the top floor, so easy access to the roof as well. I get it cheap since the last person who rented it was murdered. I live in a haunted apartment, on the top floor, in the center of the city. It's easy to find if you know what you're looking for.

I walked up the stairs and down the hallway. As I approach my door, I can see that it's already open. I stopped and held my breath. I bent down and retrieved the knife I took from Marisa from its hiding spot in my boot. I approached the doorway with the blade at the ready. I smelt the air, but the smell of alcohol and piss is too strong. I have to move carefully until I know what I'm up against.

I squeeze through the opening and close the door softly behind me. It squeaks a little but not loudly. It's pitch black inside, and I sniffed the air again, but I'm not getting anything yet. There's only one thing for me to do. I gripped my knife tight and searched the wall beside me for the light switch. I flipped it on and illuminated the room. My eyes adjusted to the brightness quickly, but there was no need for me to attack.

Instead of a group of demons sent to ambush me, I saw Marisa standing in the middle of my apartment with Ethan tied up to a chair. He is gagged, and his hands are forced behind him and handcuffed using the same hand-cuffs he used on me.

"Welcome home!" Marisa sang out, beaming at me and leaning against the chair.

"I don't even want to know how you know where I live," I said while rolling my eyes and rubbing my temples to fight off the building headache. "I do want to know how you captured him."

"That was actually the easy part," she walked over to another chair and sat down. "Once I found out he was a demon, I just tracked him down using my usual methods and shot him with a demon dart. Then I snapped my handcuffs on him, threw him in the trunk, and drove here."

I went over all the information in my head, but I could only come up with one question to ask.

"What is a demon dart?"

"It's filled with a mixture of Darkleaf berry juice, liquid magnetite, and a little bit of liquid silver. I already told you how it reacts with the demon's blood, and the Darkleaf berry juice puts them to sleep."

Ethan mumbled something through his gag, which made Marisa laugh.

"Okay," I sighed and leaned against the wall. "Why did you bring him to my apartment?"

"Ah!" She blurted out and jumped back up. "Now that's where it gets interesting. I've figured out that there was a witness that night when you were beaten to death and saved by three demons."

She dug through a bag she had hidden behind Ethan and pulled out a laptop. She placed the laptop on the counter and plugged in a flash drive.

"This is the surveillance video from the same night. It's only across the street from where you were beaten," Marisa explained as she pulled up the video from the flash drive. "We can't see the actual event, but we can see someone standing nearby watching it happen."

She played the video, and I watched as a man walked onto the street in the surveillance footage. Marisa paused it and zoomed in on the man's face. It was Ethan, there was no mistaking that. She closed the laptop, and we both turned to face the gagged and handcuffed Ethan.

I walked toward him and pulled the gag from his mouth down to his neck. He spat out a piece of cotton.

"I suggest you start talking pretty boy," Marisa growled from behind me.

Ethan scowled and narrowed his eyes at her.

"When did you start keeping pet humans, Reese?" He asked me but kept staring at her. "I hope this one's house-trained."

Marisa stomped toward him and revealed a small dagger hidden up her sleeve.

"Speak to me again, and you'll be spitting out blood along with bits of your tongue," she hissed at him while pressing the tip of the dagger against his neck.

I grabbed Marisa by the arm, but my hand slid down to her hand. It didn't matter. I just needed to get her away from Ethan. I pulled her away from him by her hand. I took her to the far corner of the room.

"Marisa, just let me handle this," I whispered to her, and we both glanced back at him. He looked angry, but differently than before. "He'll talk to me. I'll get some answers out of him."

Marisa crossed her arms, "Whatever," she mumbled.

"Alright, Ethan," I walked back to him on my own. "That's enough playing around. The only thing I want to hear coming out of your mouth right now answers my questions. Why was I there that night? What happened to me?"

Ethan smiled at me. His eyes glanced over my shoulder and Marisa, and then he sighed.

"I didn't actually see what happened to you. I arrived too late to have seen anything. All I saw were three dead demons and a puddle of human blood."

Marisa cursed under her breath, "So he's a waste of time too."

"You were there, you must have seen something!" I urged him to answer me.

"I told you, I didn't see anything, but I talked to some people who did." He shot a smug smile Marisa's way. "There was one person who saw you go down. You were outnumbered and outmatched. The demons that attacked you did it quickly and disappeared soon afterward. Shortly afterward, three different demons showed up and sacrificed themselves to keep you alive."

"Why did they do that?" I asked him only more confused even after receiving answers. "Why was I attacked like that?"

"I don't know why you were attacked yet. I think it might be because you got involved in something too big for you. I do know why they saved you." He leaned forward and looked deep into my eyes. "You're important, Reese. It was their job to keep you alive, and they did so the only way they knew how. They sacrificed their blood to give you the life you had lost. This is why I think you have lost your memories. With the blood of a demon come the memories of the demon." He paused for a moment to allow the information to sink in. "You have the memories of three other demons swimming around in there. It's no wonder you can't find your own. If you want your memories back, then you must first overcome the blood."

My knees feel weak. I need to sit down. I hurried over to the next available seat and collapsed on it. Marisa rushed to me from her corner and placed her hands on my shoulders. Ethan glared at her while she did so. I watched him look at her as if she were touching something that belonged to him, and I was reminded of another question I meant to ask.

"What about us?" I asked him, and his eyes snapped toward me. His eyebrows furrowed, begging me to ask the question again. "How are you wrapped up in all of this, exactly? I can tell by the way you talk to me and how you act around me that we have a history together. What kind of history is that?"

"It's not important," he sputtered, then sighed and lowered his head. "What happened between us is something that should never have happened. It doesn't matter now that you can't even remember me."

I looked at him and spotted a single tear form in his eye before he straightened up and returned to his usual hard exterior. He was hurt for a small moment. I could tell that much. I shook my head at the idea that he could feel anything other than hatred. I've never seen a demon with actual feelings before.

I stood up and found new strength. I was getting close to some proper information about myself and about Durin. Now all I need to do is follow my new leads.

"We need to go back to the scene of the crime," I told Marisa. "If Ethan was able to get some answers from people in the area, then maybe we can too." I looked back at Ethan. "We'll let you go for now."

He shrugged his shoulders in response.

Marisa pulled me by the arm back into the back corner of the apartment. She glanced over at Ethan then leaned in close to whisper.

"Reese, I don't trust him," she explained. "We can't let him go. One, I don't trust him to not follow us and kill us when we're not looking. Two, he still has more information about our investigation. May I remind you that you're the investigation?"

I glanced back over at Ethan, who was trying to listen to what we were saying. If his hearing is anything like mine, he can hear everything we're saying.

"Okay," I decided, "we'll bring him with us then."

11

Truth Revealed

"Marisa, you cannot walk around the city with a man in handcuffs," I shouted at her for the second time as she led Ethan around.

"I'm a detective! It is literally in my job description that I am allowed to do that," she responded while trying hard not to laugh.

I crossed my arms and stood my ground, "Marisa, take the handcuffs off. I'm sure Ethan isn't going to run off. Besides, we might need his help in a fight, and he's useless with those on."

Marisa eyed Ethan suspiciously, and he just smiled at her smugly. She let out a huge, dramatic sigh and finally took his handcuffs off. He didn't run away or attack us. He stood there and massaged his bruised wrists while still smugly smiling at Marisa.

"Right," I said triumphantly. "Let's get this over with, shall we?"

We piled into Marisa's car, and she drove us across the city to the scene where I was beaten to death all those months ago. Ethan and I could have run there, but Marisa didn't trust us alone. She also wanted to see him sitting in the cage portion of the car. We both sat up front and discussed possible reasons for the demons, sacrificing themselves for me while he remained quiet.

Marisa stopped the car on the side of the road and turned the engine off.

"This is the place," she stated. She pointed to the corner of the street. "Right around that corner is where the three demons' bodies were found."

We both open our doors and get out of the car. Marisa opens the back door for Ethan, but he doesn't get out. I leaned down to look at him.

"What's going on?"

"I can't be seen in this part of town," he responded. "Not with you. You don't need to know why. You just need to know that it will not end well for both of us if someone here spots us together."

"So, what now? You'll meet us later?"

Ethan nodded his head and remained seated. Marisa groaned and slammed the door closed.

"Guess we're on our own then," she growled as we walked away from the car.

We walked to the corner of the street, and I looked down the adjoining road. As I scanned, the road was empty, but then an image flashed past my mind, and the next thing I saw was three dead bodies lying on the floor. The vision faded, and the road was empty again. This is the place. My memories are already waking up, but it's not enough for me to know what is going on.

"Over there," Marisa pointed to a corner store across the street. "Whoever's in that store would have had a perfect view of the fight if he was here that night."

We nod at each other and head into the store. It's empty for the most part. A young boy is packing the shelves at the back and an old man sitting at the front desk. I decided that the young boy might be too young to know anything. The old man looks like he's been working here for years. He should know something.

I nudge Marisa with my elbow and gesture to the old man. She looks him up and down then nods in agreement. I walk over to him while Marisa stays close by. She keeps her eye on the boy packing the shelves and watches the front of the store.

I cleared my throat to get the old man's attention. He looked up from his newspaper, and I opened my mouth to introduce myself. Before I could say anything, his jaw dropped, and his eyes widened.

"Reese," his voice was shaky. "It's you… It's really you. You're alive." I stared at him just as shocked as he is and he rambled on. "I mean, of course, you're alive. I knew you would be. It was touch and go for a second there, but you're a strong one, aren't you? After those goons ran after you, I was sure you were dead, but you're not dead, so that's good. I mean, it is good there's no guessing involved."

I was afraid he would babble on for ages, so I threw my hand up to silence him. He put his own hand in front of his mouth as if he wouldn't be able to stop talking unless he did. My first question has already been answered. He knows me, and I've been here before. Now all I need to know is what happened that night.

"I need you to think very carefully before speaking again," I explained calmly and slowly. "I need to know what happened here the night I was attacked by those goons. What was I after? Why was I here? I was tracking something, right? What was that? Explain it to me carefully."

"I-I-I already told you all of this," he stuttered.

I'm growing impatient, and each second I spend here makes me anxious. I slammed my hand down on the counter, making him jump off his seat and back up against the wall.

"Explain it to me again!"

"Okay, okay," he cried out. "There's a meeting area in the back of the building. They come, and they have their big meetings here. I have no choice but to let them. They come one night out of the month. I let them because I have to. They're big people, big leaders, and they are not to be messed with." The man was crying now, but he kept talking. "You were tracking them down about seven months ago. You said you were going to take them down. They got the upper hand on you last time, though, so maybe play it a little safer this time, Reese."

I rolled my eyes at him. Of course, they got the upper hand on me because he probably blabbered to them with his big mouth. I can't believe old me would have trusted this guy.

"Was it Durin?" I asked him, but he seemed confused. I slammed my fist on the desk louder this time. "Was Durin there that night? Was it his men that attacked me?"

He shook his head, "Durin is much too small a fish to be playing in this pond. You know that."

Marisa stepped forward and flashed her detective's badge at him. His eyes lit up in awe when he saw it.

"I'll be needing your surveillance footage from the last year if that's possible." She instructed him.

"Oh, yes! Of course! We never delete them. We have all the tapes in the back."

"Videotapes?" Marisa asked with apparent disgust in her voice.

He nodded, and she groaned.

THE YOUNG BOY helped us carry the videotapes to the car, and we left that place. Ethan wasn't in the car when we got back, but that's okay. We don't need him for this part of the investigation. Marisa doesn't even need me for this part. I played around in her swivel chair while she reviewed the videotapes and ran some of the faces on it through the police's database.

A young police officer walked into the room, whispered something into Marisa's ear, and handed her a file. She thanked him and told him to leave. She looked through the folder then looked over at me.

"How well do you know Ethan?" she asked me, and I stopped the swivel chair.

I shrugged my shoulders, "I don't actually know him at all. I think I used to know him before I lost my memories, but at the moment, he's a distant stranger to me. Why do you ask?"

She stood up and carried the folder over to me.

"I took a picture of him and ran his face through the database, and then I did some research—well, I asked my partner to do some research on him."

"I thought I was your partner," I interrupted her, faking being hurt.

"Can you shut up and concentrate," she snapped at me. "Listen to me. Ethan's name isn't in the database, but his face is. He's not a US citizen. As far as we can tell, he was born and raised in Russia, or should I say born and trained. Whenever he enters a city, he leaves behind a long list of dead people. These are important and protected people. Whenever he is in the same city as them, they die. From this evidence, I believe that he is a hired assassin."

She pulled a paper out of the file and handed it to me.

At the top of the article is a picture of me alongside Reese's name, followed by a long list of other names.

"I also did some research on you, and it appears the same thing occurs. Your face is associated with multiple names and multiple deaths. You're also not a US citizen, but I'm not sure where you come from. The information on you only goes back about 5 years." She sat down on the desk in front of me and sighed. "However, it's clear that you, like Ethan, were a hired assassin."

I didn't say anything or disagree with her. I'm done pretending that I was innocent in my past life when all the evidence makes it clear that I wasn't. Whoever I was then, doesn't affect who I am now. I'm different. I won't let some information about my past change that.

"We can get back to this later," I eventually instructed her. "Right now, we need to figure out who those big fish are in the surveillance footage."

"My partner and I are almost finished with that," she led me across the room toward her computer and pile of papers. "From what I can tell, these are some really big players we see here. Some of these people are on the FBI's most-wanted list, and they've been after them for ages." She pointed at one of the men on the footage. "This guy is suspected of being the ring leader of a major mafia in Hong Kong. He's had a bounty on his head for ages. All of them are major players, there's no mistaking that. Here's the kicker, though." She fast-forwarded the footage and then paused it on one man's face. "This guy isn't in any database that we have. He is completely unknown, but throughout all of the footage, everyone else seems to be deferring to him. It's as if he's the boss, the biggest fish in the pond, but we have no idea who he is."

"That's a bit unsettling," I mumbled as I studied the

man's face. Something about him seemed familiar to me, but I shrugged it off.

"There's more," Marisa explained as she shuffled through some of the papers on her desk. "I went through some old reports on fights and gang wars in the city. At the moment they didn't seem that important, the same old stuff that usually goes on in this city. However, with this new information on these gang leaders and these meetings, I looked again." She placed some papers out in front of me, but I didn't bother reading them because she was going to explain them anyway. "All of the fights have always been Durin's men versus one of these guy's men, along with some unknown henchmen. I believe those unknown henchmen belong to this big fish. If you look at it with this new information, it would appear that Durin has been fighting these guys off. Reese, I know you have your own thoughts about Durin, but I think we've got him wrong. I think he's trying to help, and this guy," she pointed at the unknown man's pause frame, "he's the real problem we need to be dealing with."

12

The Blackest Blood

MARISA IS WRONG. I KNOW WHAT DURIN IS, AND HE IS genuinely evil. I know that we can't trust him no matter what the evidence appears to tell us about him. The guys in the footage are trouble as well, but I have to stick to what I know. I have to find and kill Durin.

I got into contact with Ethan like he said I should do if I need him. I told him I'm ready to go see Durin. He agrees with me and gives me a meeting place.

"You sure you won't come with me?" I asked Marisa as I prepared to leave.

She crossed her arms and shook her head. She avoided looking directly at me.

"I understand this is something you need to do," she whispered. "I have your back, you know that, but I refuse to run into this without having all the information." She glanced at me, then sighed. "If you need backup, you can always call me, but I can't guarantee I'll be able to help you with this escapade of yours."

She walked up to me. She hesitated at first, but then

she wrapped her arms around my waist and pulled me in for a hug. I leaned in and returned the hug.

"Be careful," she whispered. "I still don't trust Ethan."

I agree to be careful, say goodbye to her, and then leave. I made my way to Ethan's meeting place and wait there for him. The seething hatred I have for Durin is growing stronger by the day. I need to get to him. I only had to wait a few minutes before hearing Ethan's footsteps behind me.

"Are you sure you're ready for this?" He asked me, and I nodded in response. "I have a current location for Durin. Try and keep up."

He blurred away from me, and I rushed after him. He ran through the empty streets and dark alleyways faster than I've ever seen, but I followed right behind him. He leaped from one building to the other only to climb back down and dart down another alleyway. If I didn't know any better, I'd say he was trying to lose me. He wasn't having any luck. I was always right on his tail, but where I was working overtime to keep up, he wasn't even breaking a sweat. We stopped in a large and populated area. I was surprised to see the number of homeless people lying in their cardboard boxes and standing by trash can fires. If this was Durin's hiding spot, then I am underwhelmed.

"Excuse me, miss," an old homeless lady grabbed my arm and pulled me back. "Do you know why the fox jumps over the fence when he can dig beneath it?"

It was a strange question, but I shrugged it off as the result of an old lady losing her mind. I just smiled at her and pulled my arm free, and then I rushed off to join Ethan. Before I can get to him, we're attacked.

Suddenly the homeless people surrounding us jump up and show their true nature. They've gone full demon. They're all sporting pitch-black eyes, long dagger-like claws dipped with black ink dripping from the tip, and they're mouths are forced open by a full jaw of sharp and long teeth.

I press my back up against Ethan's, and we both stand helpless in the middle of the onslaught. This is the worst situation I've been in. I'm not about to give up now just because it looks hard. I'm willing to fight through all of them to get to Durin.

"Reese," Ethan whispered. "These are Durin's toughest men. They're his security, and they are all full demons. It's going to be hard, but you need to go full demon too. It's the only way you'll be able to match their strength."

I listened carefully, but I dreaded his advice. I've gone full demon once, by accident. When I did it, I had no control, and I was as good as a bloodthirsty monster. He is right, though. I have no choice if I want to stand a chance against them.

I closed my eyes and allowed the demon inside of me to take control. I've been using the abilities the demon blood gives me until now, but I've kept the actual demon at bay. I've kept it hidden, but now I must release it. I opened my eyes as I felt my blood boiling within. My eyes are pitch black now, I can tell by the heat coming from them and my new sight. I can see the heat pouring from everyone around me. They are red figures surrounded by black, but I don't see their faces or anything else around me. A sharp pain spread up my arm as my nails grew long and pointed. My fingertips burn as the black blood from within me, drips down to my nails' tips. It's venomous to anything it touches, that much I know. My teeth started to grow, and my jaw was forced open. All the teeth in my mouth grew too big for it and sharp enough to rip through flesh.

The transformation is complete, and the next part is all a blur to me. I know I'm killing. I know I'm slashing, clawing, biting, and slicing through the enemies around me, but I can't see it happening. I'm not in control anymore. I feel like I've done this before, but those memories and feelings are not mine. There are thousands of thoughts dancing through my mind, but none of them are mine. They belong to the demons. I am being controlled by the three demons whose blood is now running through my veins. It hurts so much, but there is nothing I can do but let it happen, and some part of me is enjoying the experience. I fight the smile pulling at my lips.

"Reese!" The voice is beside me but somewhere in the distance. "Reese it's over!" the voice is getting closer now, even though its source is right beside me. "Reese, come back to me."

My vision returns to normal, and I can see the dead bodies surrounding me. The ground is covered with the black blood of the demons I have killed. My mouth can close again, and my dagger-like nails are gone. I look up at Ethan. He is standing away from me, and he looks worried, but his eyes are wide with fear as well.

I can't think about what I've done. I need to keep my thoughts on the reason we are here in the first place.

"Take me to Durin," I instruct him.

He just stares at me for a moment, then he nods his head and leads the way into one of the buildings.

A Meeting of Enemies

We walked through the building, which looked a lot different on the inside than it did outside. It looked abandoned and falling apart on the outside. On the inside, it is clean, well maintained, and it seems like the base of Durin's operations.

Ethan led me through the almost empty building right to the top floor. When we got there, Durin was waiting for us. He stood there, and for some reason, he wasn't what I was expecting. I don't actually know what I was expecting. He was tall, skinny, and middle-aged. He looked weak, but the way he held himself with pride showed me that he was strong.

"Reese!" He sang with joy as I entered the room. He threw his arms out as if to send me a hug through the air. "I'm glad to finally see that you're okay. Why did you not answer the question? You raised the alarm, and now I've lost my whole security team."

I thought for a moment, then realized he was talking about the question the old lady asked me. It must have been a code of some kind. A code that I was supposed to know.

"It's a bit complicated," Ethan explained for me. "Her memories are being blocked by the memories of the demons' blood she now possesses."

Durin squinted his eyes at him, and his brows furrowed. He then turned to look at me, and I scowled at him. The rage is building inside me, and I'm not sure what's holding me back. I want to attack him and rip him apart. Some part of me is holding back.

"Where is the pendant?" he asks me. "Did you manage to get the pendant?"

I didn't answer him, and the confusion on my face was clear for everyone to see. He sighed and shook his head.

"This is very bad," he mumbled. "We are in a lot of trouble. Ethan, we need to get out of here, now!"

Ethan stands at attention and nods in agreement. Durin walks off, and Ethan grabs my hand. We follow after him. Ethan pulled me along as Durin led us both back through the building. I pulled my hand free of him.

"What is going on, Ethan?" I demanded, but Ethan just shook his head and grabbed my hand.

"We need to keep moving," he instructed me and pulled me along.

"I don't have a lot of time to explain," Durin spoke as we walked. "You work for Taltash, let's just say that he's the big bad guy in this area. He arrived in the city about a year ago, and he's been taking over slowly. He has everyone under his thumb. I've been trying to penetrate his organization and bring it down, but until you came along, it's been impregnable." He stopped at a computer and started typing something on the keyboard. "I don't know what you have against him. You used to be his right-hand man. He used to send you out to do his bidding. One day you came to us, and you wanted us to help you take him down. I'm not sure what turned you against him, but I was happy to help."

There is a loud bang somewhere in the building. We all turn our attention toward it. This must be why Ethan and Durin were so eager to get out of here.

"Ethan, we need to hurry," Durin whispered.

"Yes, sir," he responded.

He grabs my hand tighter, and we all start to run. I don't know where we're running to, but Durin and Ethan do. While we're running, there's a second loud bang, followed by a third. I can only assume that someone is setting off explosions in the area. The fourth loud bang came too fast and too close. The flash blinded me, and the sound left me deaf. The next thing I knew, I was on the ground surrounded by rubble. Ethan was over me and trying to say something, but all I heard was a loud, high pitched ringing sound. He dragged me along the ground. My body was limp. I allowed him to get me out of the situation because I didn't have the strength to get myself out of it.

Ethan left me to lie on the floor, and he ran to tend to

Durin. I rolled over and looked over at them. There was a lot of black blood on the floor, and I was sure it all belonged to Durin. I forced myself to stand up. I wasn't injured in any way because I wasn't feeling pain anywhere. I stumbled over to them.

"You need to get out of here," Ethan instructed me as he tended to Durin's wounds.

"Ethan, I don't understand any of this," I told him, completely ignoring his instructions. "If I was working with Durin, then why do I hate him so much? Why do I want to kill him?"

"I can't answer that," he sighed. "All I can tell you is that Durin is on your side. He's the one that instructed those demons to sacrifice themselves to save you that night. The only way you're going to get any answers is if you find your memories. You need to beat the blood inside you. I can't tell you anymore." He lifted Durin up as best he could. "I need to get his wounds mended as soon as possible. You have to get out of here before any of Taltash's men see you."

Ethan carried Durin off, and I did as he told me. I made my way out of the building, and I made sure no one saw me. I'm still not sure what's going on. I have to do what Ethan says and find my true memories.

13

A Meeting of Enemies

We walked through the building, which looked a lot different on the inside than it did on the outside. It looked abandoned and falling apart on the outside. On the inside, it is clean, well maintained, and it looks like the base of Durin's operations.

Ethan led me through the almost empty building right to the top floor. When we got there, Durin was waiting for us. He stood there, and for some reason, he wasn't what I was expecting. I don't actually know what I was expecting. He was tall, skinny, and middle-aged. He looked weak, but the way he held himself with pride showed me that he was strong.

"Reese!" He sang with joy as I entered the room. He threw his arms out as if to send me a hug through the air. "I'm glad to finally see that you're okay. Why did you not answer the question? You raised the alarm, and now I've lost my whole security team."

I thought for a moment, then I realized he was talking about the question the old lady asked me. It must have been a code of some kind. A code that I was supposed to know.

"It's a bit complicated," Ethan explained for me. "Her memories are being blocked by the memories of the demons' blood she now possesses."

Durin squinted his eyes at him, and his brows furrowed. He then turned to look at me, and I scowled at him. The rage is building inside me, and I'm not sure what's holding me back. I want to attack him and rip him apart. Some part of me is holding back.

"Where is the pendant?" he asks me. "Did you manage to get the pendant?"

I didn't answer him, and the confusion on my face was clear for everyone to see. He sighed and shook his head.

"This is very bad," he mumbled. "We are in a lot of trouble. Ethan, we need to get out of here, now!"

Ethan stands at attention and nods in agreement. Durin walks off, and Ethan grabs my hand. We follow after him. Ethan pulled me along as Durin led us both back through the building. I pulled my hand free of him.

"What is going on, Ethan?" I demanded, but Ethan just shook his head and grabbed my hand.

"We need to keep moving," he instructed me and pulled me along.

"I don't have a lot of time to explain," Durin spoke as we walked. "You work for Taltash, let's just say that he's the big bad guy in this area. He arrived in the city about a year ago, and he's been taking over slowly. He has everyone under his thumb. I've been trying to penetrate his organization and bring it down, but until you came along, it's been impregnable." He stopped at a computer and started typing something on the keyboard. "I don't know what you have against him. You used to be his right-hand man. He used to send you out to do his bidding. One day you came to us, and you wanted us to help you take him down. I'm not sure what turned you against him, but I was happy to help."

There is a loud bang somewhere in the building. We all turn our attention toward it. This must be why Ethan and Durin were so eager to get out of here.

"Ethan, we need to hurry," Durin whispered.

"Yes, sir," he responded.

He grabs my hand tighter, and we all start to run. I don't know where we're running to, but Durin and Ethan do. While we're running, there's a second loud bang, followed by a third. I can only assume that someone is setting off explosions in the area. The fourth loud bang came too fast and too close. The flash blinded me, and the sound left me deaf. The next thing I knew, I was on the ground surrounded by rubble. Ethan was over me and trying to say something, but all I heard was a loud, high pitched ringing sound. He dragged me along the ground. My body was limp. I allowed him to get me out of the situation because I didn't have the strength to get myself out of it.

Ethan left me to lie on the floor, and he ran to tend to Durin. I rolled over and looked over at them. There was a lot of black blood on the floor, and I was sure it all belonged to Durin. I forced myself to stand up. I wasn't injured in any way because I wasn't feeling pain anywhere. I stumbled over to them.

"You need to get out of here," Ethan instructed me as he tended to Durin's wounds.

"Ethan, I don't understand any of this," I told him, completely ignoring his instructions. "If I was working with Durin, then why do I hate him so much? Why do I want to kill him?"

"I can't answer that," he sighed. "All I can tell you is

that Durin is on your side. He's the one that instructed those demons to sacrifice themselves to save you that night. The only way you're going to get any answers is if you find your memories. You need to beat the blood inside you. I can't tell you anymore." He lifted Durin up as best he could. "I need to get his wounds mended as soon as possible. You have to get out of here before any of Taltash's men see you."

Ethan carried Durin off, and I did as he told me. I made my way out of the building, and I made sure no one saw me. I'm still not sure what's going on. I have to do what Ethan says and find my true memories.

14

The Heart's Confession

I DON'T TRUST WITCH DOCTORS. I THINK THEY'RE FAKE AND just looking for a quick buck. But right now, a witch doctor seems to be my only option if I want to awaken my memories and figure out my past.

"Have you ever done something like this before?" The witch doctor asked me while I sat down on one of the pillows on the floor.

I shook my head and examined the teapot in front of me. The steam coming out of it smelt strange, but I tried to ignore it.

"It's fairly simple," he explained. "I will give you some of this special tea," he poured some in the glass in front of me. "Once you drink it, the special chemicals will begin to work at unlocking your mind. It will seem strange at first, but everything will start to make sense once you have passed the first stage."

I picked up the cup and smelt the tea again. This is not your ordinary English tea, and I didn't even want to think about what is actually inside it. I looked up at the witch doctor, and he just smiled and nodded his head.

"Here goes nothing," I sighed and took a sip of the tea.

It tastes foul and burns my throat, but I keep drinking until the cup is empty. I put the cup down and forced the last bit down my throat. I exhale loudly as the tea boiled in my stomach.

I intended to ask the witch doctor what I needed to do next, but something stopped my tongue from moving. It felt numb and heavy at the same time. I opened my mouth, but then it felt like I couldn't close it again. The bottom half of my jaw stretched all the way to the ground, and I couldn't lift it back up.

The walls around me began to twist, dance, and change color. The floor swirled around like a pool, and my body began melting into it. I looked up at the witch doctor, and his eyes turned a glowing red, and he started laughing at me. His laugh was deep and echoed through the room. I tried to scream as the floor swallowed me up, but I couldn't make a sound. All I could hear was the witch doctor's laugh. All I could see was my body melting into the swirling floor. I cried out as everything went black.

I opened my eyes, and the light was blinding. I was out of my body and floating through the air. It was as if I was watching a movie while still being in the movie. I watched a little girl, and even though I didn't know who she was, I knew she was me.

A tall man knelt down in front of her, and he smiled a gentle giant's smile. He hands her a gift as I float above him.

"Happy birthday, my little warrior," he spoke, and it was but an echo of words spoken long before.

The little girl jumped up and down and cheered. She took the present. A long box the size of her small forearm, and she opened it. Inside was a silver dagger with a black jeweled hilt. She lifted it from the box, and the handle fit perfectly in her hand. The silver metal caught the light of the sun and blinded me for a moment.

When I opened my eyes again, the little girl was taller and a bit older. She held the knife out in front of her and copied the movements of the man beside her. He showed her how to move it and how to move her body. She followed every move he made perfectly. He smiled at her with pride and joy. They faced each other and bowed their heads slightly.

"I am impressed, little one," the man spoke. "No student of mine has learned as quickly and efficiently as you."

"Please, Taltash," the girl said. "Don't call me little one anymore. I am a grown woman now."

"Indeed you are," he stepped forward and wrapped his arms around the girl. "You will always be a little girl to me. My little warrior."

The girl's life flashed in front of me. Images of times in her life flew by almost too fast for me to see. I saw the man sitting with her and helping her write something. I watched them run around a vast garden playing tag with some other men dressed in black. The more I watched, the more I came to terms with the fact that this girl was me, and these were images of my life. Taltash isn't an evil man. From what I can tell, he is my father or the only father I have ever known or had.

More images flashed past, faster and faster until I couldn't tell one from the other or make out what was happening. I looked up to see a large brick wall in front of me. I was flying toward it at high speed, and there was no way to stop myself. I closed my eyes as I slammed into the wall.

I gasped and shot up out of my seat. Whatever was inside that tea has worn off, and I can stand up straight now without the world spinning around me. I looked down to see the witch doctor. I must have been in my trance for long because he has fallen asleep in his seat. I left some money in my seat and went on my way. I didn't learn all I needed to know, but I learned enough to know that Durin is still the enemy, and Taltash might actually be the man who raised me.

"I DON'T KNOW how to explain it," I confessed to Marisa. "It was like a dream, but the dream was real. It was a dream about my life, and I was floating above it all, seeing things through my own eyes and not the eyes of my younger self."

"You drank strange tea given to you by a strange man," Marisa spoke like a zombie, and she was starting to sound like one since she has repeated that sentence four times. "It's a wonder you weren't murdered during your little memory dream."

"He was a professional witch doctor, Marisa," I reminded her. "How else do you expect me to unlock my memories?"

"I don't think the word professional, and the title witch doctor go together."

"Marisa!" I wanted to be angry, but I couldn't help laugh a little, and Marisa joined in on my giggling. "Are you going to help me or not?"

"Okay," she said while still giggling. "I'll see what I can find on this Taltash guy."

She opened up her laptop and started clicking at the keyboard like a mad person. Her fingers danced across the keys faster than I imagined was possible. She was used to this kind of work. She does it all the time, and she's perfected it.

I got up off my seat and walked up behind her. I put my hands down on her shoulders and leaned forward to see what she's doing. I'm not that interested in her work, though. I just wanted to get closer to her. I'm not sure why, but Marisa is interesting to me. I've been around a lot of humans since I woke up in the hospital, but Marisa is nothing like any of them. She is strong in a way that even I'm not. She is not physically stronger than me, but her mind is stronger than mine. She has the determination to do things that I would hesitate to do, and she is committed to seeing things through. I can admire that kind of strength.

I still don't know why she wants to help me or what she sees in me. Perhaps one day she'll tell me why. Until that day, I must assume that she sees me the same way she sees everyone else; a means to an end. I could also ask her. That is a question that's easier to ask in the mind than to force out of my mouth.

I caught her glancing up at me as her typing slowed down. I glanced down at her, and our eyes meet. She quickly pulls her gaze away and returns to her typing. Just before she pulled away from me, I saw her cheeks turn pink. I pulled up a chair and sat next to her. This seemed to make her even more uncomfortable than when I was standing over her.

I leaned over onto her chair and rested my elbow on her chair's arm. My head was practically resting on her shoulder while I watched her type. I felt her arm tense up for a moment. Eventually, she relaxed and returned to her work. This felt comfortable for me. I can tell that Marisa likes it as well, even though she would hate to admit it.

"According to this, the name Taltash is probably a

fake," she spoke to break the silence. "The only thing I can find on that name happened ages ago. I'm talking over a century ago. The name is probably a fake one, but I did a search on the description you gave me. Tall, pale, an old face but not old enough to be sporting any wrinkles, shoulder-length black hair, and wearing some old Japanese looking robes."

"That's what he looked like in my memories," I agreed with her. "However, I was pretty young in those memories, so I'm not sure if he still looks that way."

"We can keep our fingers crossed."

I stared at her while she did some more work, and a question burned inside my mind. The more I ignored the question, the hotter it got. It moved its way down to my throat and sat on the tip of my tongue. It threatened to force my mouth open and jump out at her. I needed to ask the question now while I'm still in control. If I don't and the question forces itself out, I may sound crazy.

"Do you like me?"

Marisa froze and stopped working. She turned to face me, her eyes wide, and her brows furrowed with confusion and shock.

"What kind of question is that?" her voice was shaky and cute in a way.

"It's a perfectly normal question," I explained. "You're so closed off and shut away that I can't tell if you like me or not. I can't tell what you're thinking at all. All I can tell is that you care about your work and at the moment I'm your work. I know you care about me in that way, but do you care about me in any other way?"

She pushed her chair away from her laptop and slightly away from me, but she did it so she could face me. She put her hands up as if she wanted to slow me down, or she wanted me to stop talking.

"This is a lot of information to take in at once, okay," she eventually said. "Let me think for a second." She took a deep breath and looked straight at me. "Of course I like you. I wouldn't be helping you if I didn't. I've been watching you for months, getting to know you, and that has an effect on a person. You're a mystery to me, and I like that. I like solving mysteries. You don't have to worry, Reese, okay, I do like you." She turned back to her laptop. "Stop making things awkward. Kind of makes it hard to work."

I smiled, and I couldn't stop. It wasn't exactly the answer I was looking for, but it was better than what I was expecting. Her laptop made a noise.

"We've got a search result back on the man's description," she said and typed a bit more. "This guy Taltash has been spotted in the city once before around a year ago. Around the same time, some guy's henchmen started attacking Durin's men."

"It's the same guy then," I stated.

"There's more," she opened up so many documents on her laptop I wondered how she knew what was going on. "This guy's face has been spotted all over the city during important events. He's been seen shaking hands with politicians, doing deals with massive companies, and basically getting his hands into a lot of pots. This guy owns half the city!"

"That's a bad thing, I'm guessing."

"No one man should have this much power," she explained, "especially a man like this guy. Ever since he came into the city, there has been a series of strange deaths and disasters. These are deaths of big people with a lot of power, and these disasters seem to kill a lot of random people while destroying a huge part of the city."

"You think he is behind it all?" I couldn't believe it. Not

the man who raised me and acted like such a good man in my memories.

"I'm not sure," she shrugged her shoulders, "but it's a big enough coincidence to be suspicious. According to my research, this area of the city seems to be his main territory. I suggest we go down there and see what we can get out of the locals."

Marisa drives us to the center of the city. This is the heart of the city. Where all the big businesses are and where the streets are the busiest. I would have gotten here faster if I was allowed to run, but Marisa insisted she drive us. She wants to keep a low profile. I can agree with that, but cars are so slow and annoying to me. We eventually arrive, and I free myself of the car.

Marisa leads the way down the street. It's Marketplace street. Not its actual name, but that's what everyone calls it because every day of the week, except Sunday, it is turned into a marketplace. Vendors set up along the sidewalk and work hard to sell their goods. Some are handmade, others are brought in bulk and sold at a markup, and some people also just sell food.

Both our stomachs were growling so loudly we decided to get some hotdogs. Marisa ordered for me and paid. It felt like a date. I wouldn't tell her that, given how she'd freaked out at my earlier question.

As we walked along, several people stepped forward and gave us their best pitches. They were all very eager to sell us something. I ignored most of them and kept walking. I stopped every now and again to look at a pretty necklace or an interesting plate. One lady who resembled a gypsy caught my eye with a bracelet.

"How much?" I asked as I eyed the silver bracelet with purple dolphin-shaped jewels threaded in the chain.

The gypsy lady smiled and winked at me, "Any price you'd like."

I gave her what I had on me and took the bracelet. It was an odd reply, but I didn't think much of it. Gypsy women are always strange. I caught up with Marisa and hid the bracelet in my pocket. An old man walked toward me and asked me a question. I ignored him and continued walking beside Marisa. However, Marisa stopped and stared at the old man. I watched her brow furrow, and her eyes squint as she scanned the area we just left behind.

She grabbed my hand and pulled me into a nearby alleyway. We were alone now, away from the marketplace and all the people.

"What's going on?" I asked her.

"There's something strange about the questions they were asking us," she replied. "I think they were talking in code."

"What makes you think that? They were all just trying to sell us something."

"Weren't you listening?" she raised her voice in evident irritation at me. "Four people asked you the same question. The old man just did it now. They completely bypassed me and walked straight to you and asked you the same question. They all called you a little warrior."

I gasped, "That's what Taltash called me in my memories." I glanced back at the street we left behind us. "He's trying to reach out to me."

15

The Awakening

THE COUCH WAS COMFORTABLE ENOUGH TO TAKE A NAP ON. Still, I wasn't feeling comfortable enough to actually take a nap. The hypnosis therapist stood over me, and Marisa sat in a chair in the corner. She was smiling at me. It was supposed to be reassuring having her here, but I don't feel reassured.

"This is a stupid idea," I muttered then raised my voice so Marisa could hear me. "This is a really dumb idea!"

"You want to unlock your memories, don't you?" She sighed. "This is a lot less dumb than drinking mushroom tea from a witch doctor."

"I disagree with this."

The hypnotist stood over me, hanging a pocket watch over my face. She gave me instructions, and I followed them. Marisa went silent, and only the hypnotist's voice made its way into my mind.

"You are getting sleepy," she said, and I was reminded of a movie I once watched. "Focus on the watch. Notice its color, its shape, and try to imagine its weight in your hand.

Focus on that, and your mind will be calm. You are getting sleepy…"

My eyes felt as heavy as I imagined the watch was. Its round shape was perfect, and its gold trim caught the light. The world around me faded into black as my eyes fell closed.

I wasn't asleep, but my eyes felt like they were closed shut. I can't remember what was happening around me or what was happening inside my head. Memories floated past me. Most of them were unimportant, or they moved past me too fast for me to see them. They were all still there, though. I couldn't watch them now, but they were in my mind. It's as if they were being unlocked and thrown at me.

I feel uncomfortable now. It's black around me, and I feel like I'm falling through an endless space. Something's chasing me, I don't know what it is, and I don't want to find out. I scream and punch and kick. The next thing I hear is Marisa's voice, and I feel a hand on my chest.

My eyes snap open, and I jump up off of the couch I was recently chained to. Marisa is standing beside me, her eyes wide with fear. Her eyes aren't nearly as wide as the hypnotist's eyes are.

"What the hell happened?" Marisa asked me.

My heart was pounding in my chest, but it felt like it fell to the stomach's pit. I'm not sure why I freaked out. I just felt uncomfortable. I felt like I was somewhere I shouldn't be. Like there is some part of my mind, I'm not allowed to go in.

"I'm not sure," I replied once my breathing was back to normal. "I got a few memories there. I need to be some-where. I'm supposed to be somewhere tonight."

I GAVE Marisa the address from my head, and she drove us there. It's a hotel and quite a fancy one as well. I know that the apartments are above, and there is a club below. The club is hosting a gala, and I have to attend it. First, I need to go to my apartment in the building above. I'm not sure how I came to know all this, I just know it.

My room number is 761. I head straight there with Marisa following behind me. I'm walking with a new sense of pride. There are courage and certainty in my step, and I hold my head up high. I feel confident. I feel like this place is where I belong, at least for the night.

A man is standing in front of the apartment door, and he looks our way. Marisa starts to panic, but I keep my cool. This man knows who I am, and he will let me in. Somehow I just know that.

"Good evening Reese," the man speaks as he bows his head slightly to me.

"Good evening," I respond. "Is everything ready for tonight?"

He nods his head, "Everyone is waiting for you to join the party."

I thank him, and he takes his leave. I knew exactly what to say to him, and that scares me. The words were coming off my tongue, but it didn't feel like my words. It didn't feel like my tongue. We go inside the apartment.

"I assume you're getting your memories back," Marisa spoke once the door was closed behind us.

I shrugged my shoulders, "I'm not sure about that. I know what I'm supposed to do in the moment, but I can't remember why I'm supposed to do it. I just know that I'm supposed to be here, I'm supposed to say those things, and I'm supposed to go to the gala tonight."

I headed toward the walk-in closet and through one of the closet doors. Somehow I knew it would be full. These are my clothes, but I don't remember putting them here. I just knew that they were here. I feel that this was my actual apartment before I lost my memories, but I'm not sure, and I won't tell Marisa that.

I pick one dress out of the closet and put it out on the bed, then I choose a pair of shoes to match. The dress will come just above my knees and have a small slit in the side to about midway up my thigh. It will look sexy and give me movement if I need it. It's a dark purple color with a black swirling pattern on one half. The black swirls appear to take the shape of flowers if you look close enough. The shoes are plain black heel boots that will go past my ankles.

"You're going to the gala then," Marisa seemed disappointed when she spoke.

"I have to go," I told her. "I need to find out what's going on, and somehow it is tied to this event tonight. I think it's important."

"I guess I'll try and give you some backup then," she sighed. "I'll stay up here and wait. You can call me if you need me."

I smiled at her and walked to the closet. I grabbed a dress that would match mine and handed it to her.

"Actually, I think I would prefer it if you come to the gala as my plus one."

Marisa didn't say anything, but I could tell by how she smiled that I made her very happy. We both got dressed and prepared ourselves for the event. It's a good thing, Marisa, and I are the same size, even if she is a bit shorter than me. Short dresses on me will be modest dresses on her. That's not a big deal. We came up with a plan and some code words, and then we made our way down to the gala.

We pass several people along the way to the party, and each one stops to ask me a question. Something inside me immediately knows that they are asking me for passwords. I answer every single one of them. I don't remember what they asked me and I don't remember any of my answers. It's as if I'm being controlled. I'm doing and saying all of these things, but it doesn't feel like it's me. I feel like I'm trapped in my own mind, and I have to go along for the ride for any of this to work. I give every single person that talks to me a code. This code means everything is fine and that they should all proceed per usual. Now all I have to do is figure out what they're moving with.

Marisa walks with me the whole way and hangs on my arm. I can tell that she feels just as uncomfortable as me. I'm just better at hiding it right now. She holds onto me tightly as we enter the gala. I look around, and I immediately smell something familiar.

I look up at the area above us, separated by a spiral staircase and some glass banisters, to see Ethan and Durin looking down at us. Ethan seems worried, and Durin just smiles at me. I let out a long sigh.

"Ethan and Durin are here," I whisper to Marisa.

"Great!" She mutters. "Reese, do you have any idea what you're doing?"

I look around us at all the people, some faces seem familiar, and others don't. I don't see the one face I'm looking for and a knot forms in my stomach.

"No," I reply. "I have no idea what I'm doing."

16

The Kiss of Life and the Moment of Death

THE EVENING ROLLED BY SLOWLY AS MARISA AND I CHOSE to mingle with the crowd to blend in. Durin and Ethan watched us from above. They kept a low profile as well. I guess they also know something big is about to go down, and either they're here to stop it or start it. I'm not sure.

All the confidence I had when entering this situation faded away quickly. The memories have stopped flashing into my mind, and now I don't know what I'm supposed to do. I don't know what is supposed to happen. I know that I'm supposed to be at this gala, and I'm supposed to do something important.

"Reese," Marisa whispered in my ear as she wrapped her arm around mine. "I suggest we leave. The situation has gotten out of hand, and we're no longer in control. Unless you get yourself some new memories about what's supposed to happen tonight, we should get out of here."

"Not yet," I muttered and almost growled at her. "This is important! I don't know why yet, but we need to stay and figure it out."

"Then figure it out!"

She spoke through gritted teeth, and I've never seen her speak that way before. She's on edge. She should be, I guess. We could be in the middle of a lot of bad men and not even know it. She pulls away from me, and we separate once again. She combs the left side of the dance floor, and I search the right. I want to go upstairs, but the stairs are guarded, and I'm sure they require a password. I don't have that password yet.

An image flashes into my mind, and I have to sit down before I lose my balance. More images flash. They burn in my mind and force me to close my eyes so I can see them clearer. I see the gala and people taking their positions around the dance floor. I see myself taking my position at the edge of the dance floor with the bar behind me. The images fade, and I'm able to stand again. I look around me and realize that I'm standing at the bar now. Some of the people in the flashing images have already taken their positions.

Something is going to go down, and it's going down now. I push away from the bar and walk toward the dance floor. If my memories are correct, then this is the place I'm supposed to stand. I stand in between the dance floor and the bar, and I immediately feel eyes on me. They're staring. My knees feel weak, and I want to run away, but I have to see this through if I want to know what's going on.

"Oh, I'm sorry, dear," an old man said as he bumped into me from behind.

I stumbled forward but caught myself and rebalanced, "That's alright."

He looked into my eyes and spoke with a blank face, "Do you know why the sparrow chooses to fly south?"

I stared at him with squinted eyes and a furrowed brow. He waited only a few seconds for an answer. When I didn't give him one, he apologized and walked away. As he left, I realized it was a code, and I didn't answer. I didn't know the answer. It was a test, and I failed. In an instant, I had eyes burning holes into my body. They know that I'm an intruder. I have no idea what my answer was supposed to be, and I have no idea what is supposed to happen now.

My heart is pounding in my ears, and a knot is forming in my stomach. I left my position and searched the gala for Marisa. I spot her long brown hair and rush toward her. She's in a conversation with a young woman, but I excuse her and pull her away. She's angry, but that doesn't matter.

"We've been made," I whispered in her ear as I walked her into a quiet area at the front of the gala. "Someone asked me a question. It was a coded message, but I didn't know the answer."

"Great!" She growled, bared her teeth, and looked around. She noticed the many eyes on us as well.

My eyes are drawn to a man entering the dance floor from across the way. I stare at him for a while, and for some reason, I remember seeing his face before. My head starts to hurt, and I dig my nails into Marisa's arm. She holds me up even though I want to double over and collapse from the pain. Everything goes white, and an image flashes into my mind.

Someone hands me a picture, and I look at it. It's an image of the man who is on the dance floor now. He is a major politician playing big games with prominent people. I stare at the picture and smile.

"I'm supposed to kill him?" I ask as if the act is an insult. "When and where?"

"There is going to be a gala in a few months, and he will be invited." I hear a familiar voice echo in my mind. "Your job is to make it look like a hit. I want someone to know that he was killed for a reason. Then we can blame it on Durin and his men."

I smile and look up to see Taltash standing beside me and smiling back. The image fades, and so does the pain. I stand up and look around. I don't know if anyone noticed, but Marisa did an excellent job keeping me on my feet. If I was alone, I would be rolling on the ground.

"I know what's supposed to happen," I muttered as I struggle to catch my breath. "That man over there on the dance floor, he's supposed to die." I pointed to the politician that's just entered the dance floor. "He's a major politician working on the development of poverty-stricken areas in the city. That's why I'm supposed to be here. I'm supposed to kill him."

Marisa released me from her grip and made a grab at her purse. Inside her purse is a small, police issued handgun. She brought it just in case, even though I told her not to. Something stopped her from grabbing the gun, though. She relaxed again and let out a small, soft laugh.

"That's great then," she whispered. "If you're supposed to kill him, then we don't need to worry."

"Why not," I almost yelled at her but managed to keep my voice down.

"Well, you're not going to kill him, are you," she elbowed me playfully and smiled. "Unless you have the sudden urge to kill someone, the politician should be safe."

She's right. I don't have the urge to kill anyone except Durin, but I've always had that urge. It's my job to kill the politician, but I'm not going to do it. However, I have a feeling that Taltash is smarter than that. I get the feeling that he's one of those men that when he wants something done, it gets done.

I feel a pair of eyes staring down at me, and I look up. My heart stops beating for a moment, and I swallow hard. Marisa follows my eyes, and soon we're both staring at him. Taltash is standing at the top floor of the gala, looking down at me. If it weren't for my awakened memories, I wouldn't know who he is, but something tells me that I would still suspect. I know him. I remember him in a more profound way than I know anyone else in this room, even without all of my memories.

He has a puzzled look plastered on his face as he stares at me. I smile and wave at him. I don't know if that's what I'm supposed to do, but I don't know what else there is to do. It's clear I've done the wrong thing when he shakes his head at me. His face turns sour and angry. I don't know what to do, and I'm afraid of what he'll do if he realizes that I'm not the Reese he knows.

Suddenly I feel Marisa's hand grip mine. She pulls me toward her and swoops me down. I feel her second hand press against the small of my back as she leans my head back. She looks into my eyes for a second before pressing her lips against mine. Her lips are wet with lip gloss, and they smell of berries. I'm shocked for a moment, but it feels nice. It's a feeling I'm not used to, and yet it's familiar. I twist my head to the side and push into her lips. I would like this moment to last a little longer, but it only lasted a few seconds.

Marisa pulls away from me, and I stand up straight. I'm still holding her hand tight, and she's not pulling away. I smile at her slightly, but she doesn't smile back. She's scanning the room. I snap out of it and get my head back in the game. I glance back up at Taltash, but he isn't there anymore. I then turn my attention to the politician on the dance floor.

He has a drink in his hand, and he's speaking with a few people. This is it. This is the moment I'm supposed to kill him. He is vulnerable and within my sights. That is if I was in my position at the edge of the dance floor with the bar at my back.

"Someone else is going to do it," Marisa informs me, snapping me out of my thoughts.

"How can you be sure?"

She points at the spot where I'm supposed to be standing, and now someone else is standing there. Taltash does have a backup plan. He must not trust me as much as everyone thinks he does.

"We need to protect the politician," Marisa orders. "You handle the man who took your place. I'll try to get the politician out of here without drawing any attention."

I nod in agreement, and we split up. Marisa heads around to the back of the dance floor, where she can grab the politician easily. I head toward the man standing in my position.

Blood is rushing to my ears, and my heart is in the pit of my stomach. My mind is racing with everything that's happened tonight. Seeing Taltash, finding out I'm supposed to kill someone, and kissing Marisa. It's all running around inside my head. I can't concentrate on all of them at once, but I can't push the memories down.

As I'm on my way to stop the new killer, but people get in my way. They stumble in front of me, knock into me, try to push me over, and deliberately stop me to ask me something. I try to push past all of them, but they're slowing me down. This is the plan. They're all working for Taltash, and their jobs are to protect the killer from any interference. I manage to glance over at Marisa, and I can see the same thing is happening to her. I need to move faster, but the crowd in front of me is getting thicker.

I look at the politician as someone moves behind him and pushes him. He stumbles forward into the center of the dance floor and drops his drink. The glass shatters on the floor as the killer raises his arm. He's holding a gun. I'm done playing games. I push past the people, flinging some of them into the air and pushing others down to the ground. I rush toward the killer with my hands out, ready to tackle the gun away from him. Before I can reach him, his finger tightens around the trigger, and he pulls it.

The rest happened so fast. The bang from the gun was loud enough to fill the whole room. Those who weren't a part of the operation didn't hesitate to scream, duck, and run for their lives. Those who were part of the operation stood still for a moment, and they all stared at the politician. He fell to the floor instantly with a bullet hole in his head. Once they were sure the job was done, and he was dead, they joined the crowd of screaming citizens.

They pushed past me, but I just stared at the body on the floor as a puddle of blood spread out from his head. It made me sick to my stomach. I've seen blood before, and I've killed people before. I've killed demons who worked for bad men doing bad things. I've never killed an innocent human who didn't even see it coming.

Marisa pulled her gun out of her purse and rushed to the entrance. She flashed her badge and instructed the guards to close the doors and let no one leave. Some people had already made their way out. I was sure that all of Taltash's men were gone, except for me, of course.

One thought burns in my mind, and I rush toward the spiral staircase. I need to get to Taltash. He's behind all of this, and I need to get to him. I reach the top floor and look around. I was sure he might be gone already, but I have no choice but to try. I hear a door squeak open, and my head snaps in the direction of the sound. There he is. I see Taltash by the fire escape, and he turns around to look at me.

He looks disappointed but also surprised. I don't care how he feels about me. All I care about is the dead politician on the floor downstairs and how his blood is on my hands in so many ways. I bare my teeth at him, and he closes the door behind him.

I rush toward the door and pull it open. The hall on the other side of the door is empty, but I run down it anyway. He must be fast. I make it to the end of the hall, and there is another door that is just about to close. He must have gone through there. I pull the door open and run out. I run out into the open air, and I'm stopped by a metal railing.

I'm standing at the top of a metal staircase leading down to the street. I look around, and it's dark, cold, and wet. Most importantly, the street is empty. I can't see or smell anyone. Taltash was here, but I've lost him. How could he be so fast that I can't even keep up with him? I haven't met anyone faster than me up until now.

There's no point in me staying out in the cold or looking for him when I don't know where he's gone. I head back inside to look for Marisa. I make my way to the dance floor, and my eyes fall on the dead politician again. It makes me sick. I felt Marisa's hand on my shoulder, and she forced me to look away from the dead politician.

"Reese listen to me," she spoke softly and clearly. "You need to get out of here. I don't want you anywhere near the crime scene, okay."

"Why?" I asked her, but I felt like a zombie as I spoke. "Do you not trust me?"

She opened her mouth to answer, but she hesitated. I pulled away from her because that was all the answer I needed. I pushed passed the crowd toward the door, and Marisa told the guards to let me leave.

I made my way home with a new feeling burning in my chest. I've never felt this feeling before, but I know what it is. It's a broken heart.

17

The Darkest Night

MY HOME USED TO BE A SAFE PLACE FOR ME TO COME TO. I would feel comfortable there, and I would allow myself a moment of peace and relaxation. It was a safe haven. Not tonight. Tonight, my home is a dark and lonely place that opens up my mind to all the things that I did wrong tonight.

It would be less dark if I turned the lights on. I close the door behind me and raise my hand to the light switch. Something stops me. I don't need the light because I belong in the dark. The events tonight have shown me that my heart is just as black as my blood. I decide to keep the lights off because I don't deserve them. I deserve to be consumed by the darkness that is within and around me.

I don't understand any of it. How could I have been so stupid to think I was anything other than a monster? It was my job to kill that man tonight. I remember seeing the picture and being told what I was supposed to do to him. I remember smiling at the thought. I was a killer. I'm still a killer. Perhaps I'm no better than Durin, Taltash, and all their men.

I collapse onto the couch and rub my hands across my face. My face feels itchy for some reason. As if it doesn't belong to me, and I need to pull it off. I don't know who I am anymore. I'm not Reese, and I'm not whoever I was before Reese. I'm no one.

I still don't understand why my memories haven't all come back yet. I've done everything I can possibly do. They started coming back. I was so confident earlier tonight, and I knew who I was. All of that went away, and I was lost again in a pool of memories that don't belong to me.

I don't want to feel sad. I want to be angry at myself. I can't help the flood of tears flowing from my eyes and drenching the couch pillows beneath me. I bit down on my tongue. I might not be able to control my tears, but I can control my voice. I would rather silently cry in the dark than allow anyone to hear my sorrow.

I'm not sure how long I was lying there in my own salty tears. I'm not sure when Ethan entered the room. The next thing I knew, he picked me up and pulled me into his body. He wrapped his arms around me, and I buried my tear-stained face in his chest. His touch was soothing enough to stop my tears, but it wasn't enough to calm my anger at myself.

I pushed away from him and curled up at the end of the couch. I pulled my knees up to my chest and wrapped my arms around my legs to hold them there. I felt safe in this position. I let the anger and sorrow form a big ball in the pit of my stomach, and I let it burn there.

"Reese," Ethan whispered. "Talk to me. Tell me what's going on inside that head of yours."

"Why do you care?" I muttered in response. "Why does anyone care what a monster is thinking?"

"You're not a monster."

"I don't know what I am," I snapped at him and raised my voice. "I don't know who I used to be or who I'm supposed to be. I'm nothing!"

"I know who you used to be." He moved closer to me. "I used to know you well. Your favorite color was purple. You liked drinking tea in the morning when you woke up. You used to say you only take two sugars, but you would sneak three in when I wasn't looking. I know a lot about you, Reese. If you want to know who you used to be, all you have to do is ask."

"Is that all you remember about me? I used to put three sugars in my tea?"

"No!" He stood up in front of me. "I used to love the way you would assess a situation. Whenever we went on a mission together, you would be detached and emotionless. It was something I admired about you. Not many humans can just turn their emotions off the way you did."

I shook my head and made a disgusted sound, "I'm not that person anymore."

He got down on his knees and took my hand in his.

"No, you're not," he whispered as he stared into my eyes. No matter how dark it is in here, our demon sight allowed us to see each other. "At first I couldn't believe it was possible, but it is. Even with the demon blood inside you, you're more human now than you ever were when you were actually human. The demon blood is bringing out your humanity, and it's intoxicating. I liked the woman you were before, but I think I love the women you are now." He squeezed my hands. "I, for one, am really looking forward to seeing the person you're becoming."

I pulled my hand away from him and looked away. It doesn't matter if he likes who I'm becoming. What matters is if I can live with the person I am and the person I used to be.

"Get some rest," he instructs me as he stands up. "I'll be back in the morning, and we can decide what our next move will be."

I watch him leave, and I allow my thoughts to return to the encompassing darkness. I'm alone, and that's good. I need to pull myself out of this, and I need to do it alone.

18

Pure Blood

It took the sun shining through my open window for me to realize the next day had arrived. The night is over, but the memories and feelings are still there. I don't remember falling asleep, but I spend the whole night lying on the couch. I made my decision sometime in the night, but the deal was sealed when the warmth of the sun touched my face.

I jumped up off the couch and got to work. I need to clean myself up and get out of this stupid dress before Ethan gets here. I have a new purpose and a new fire. Now more than ever, I'm determined to bring down Durin. It's the only thing I know for sure. Last night I tried to do something else, but I failed because that is not me anymore. I need to kill Durin. I still don't know why, but I know that the need to do it is stronger now than ever.

I just finished getting dressed when I heard the front door open. Ethan is here. I cursed myself for not locking the door last night. That is the kind of mistake I can't afford to make any more. I walked out into the lounge to meet him.

"Are you feeling better?" He asked me while leaning against the counter in the kitchen. He had his arms crossed, and he kept his eyes on me.

I nodded my head, "Better and ready to get the job done."

"Good!" He pushed himself away from the counter and walked toward me. "I found some information about Taltash to help us figure out what our next step will be."

"What about Durin?"

"Durin's not the problem right now. Taltash is the one we need to worry about, and we need to work together with Durin to stop him."

I rolled my eyes and sighed at him, which only made him furrow his brow at me. I obviously disagreed with him, but there was no need to argue now. I decided to listen to the information. Everything he told me seemed bad at first. Everything that Taltash does whenever he enters a city or a town is all horrible things. If you don't think about it too much. Everything Ethan tells me about him seems bad, but the longer I think about it, it doesn't seem that bad anymore.

Whenever he enters a city, a rising death-toll follows. Poverty-stricken people are killed, and parts of the city are destroyed. However, after the destruction comes creation. The places of the city that were destroyed are quickly replaced by something better and brighter. The city's poverty rate goes down. It seems to me that Taltash bleeds out the bad in the city to build up something better.

"Do you see it now?" Ethan asks me after finishing off his rant about Taltash. "Do you see now why we have to take him down?"

"If you want my honest opinion," I paused to allow him to answer, and he nodded his head. "No, I don't see what the big deal is."

He opened his mouth to protest, but before he could say a word, the front door opened, and I again cursed myself for not locking it. Marisa walked in with her laptop bag on her back and cradling a pile of files in her arms. She looked up and froze like a deer in headlights. Ethan and I stared at her for a moment before she kicked the door closed behind her.

"Am I too late for the party?" She joked as she placed the files on the kitchen counter beside Ethan.

Ethan pushed off the counter to get away from her. I watched him take out his phone and type something into it. I leaned over to try to see the screen, but he put it away as quickly as he took it out.

"I have some information on Taltash," Marisa started, but Ethan interrupted her by laughing. "Do you have a problem?" She shot a look of death at him.

"I don't think any information is going to work because miss half-demon here doesn't think we should be going after Taltash."

Marisa spun around and stared at me with wide eyes and a slightly open jaw. Ethan kept his disapproval look, but now it was mixed with a look of pain as if I hurt him in some way.

"Reese, I don't think you fully understand how this guy operates," Marisa stated. She grabbed a few files and handed them to me. "He doesn't just kill thousands of people and destroy whole cities if it suits him. He owns the city itself." Ethan and I furrowed our brows at her, so she explained. "People go missing, or they are killed at random. Important people like that politician last night. Then they are replaced by someone who Taltash can control. That politician has already been replaced along with several other important and high-ranking people in the city. I hate to admit it, but even the police captain has been replaced by someone who works for Taltash."

"That would explain why the entire police force has been focusing its efforts on Durin these past few months." Ethan walked over to the files and started looking through them. "Taltash must have instructed the new captain to keep everyone fixed on Durin. This keeps Durin busy and keeps Taltash in the dark."

"Exactly!" Marisa smiled as if she had found an old friend in Ethan.

I stood there and watched the two of them get along for the first time since they met. It should be a heart-warming moment, but it's not. The longer I think about it, the more sense it makes. Taltash is doing something good for this city. Why am I the only one that sees that? Am I blind because I used to work for him? Am I ignoring the obvious because of my uncontrollable hatred for Durin?

"The police captain is the least of our problems as well," Marisa continued, "If my data is correct, then Taltash not only owns the mayor but also the governor."

"That's not good." Ethan began pacing. "He's had a whole year to work on this. What does he have planned for the city? Why bother gaining all this control?"

"I don't care what his plan is. We need to stop him before we get the chance to find out."

The hatred inside me is building. I don't understand why they hate Taltash so much. He doesn't sound that bad to me. Yes, he's killed people, but so have I, and so has Ethan, and I'm sure Marisa has killed as well. He doesn't seem like a monster to me. He comes into a city and eradicates the poisonous tissue so the rest of the city can heal.

Durin is the problem. We should be going after him. I need to kill him. That's all I know, and that's all I want to know. He needs to be brought to justice for everything he has done.

"Are you with us, Reese?" Marisa asks, but I can barely hear her.

My teeth are bared, my fists are clenched, and I'm ready for a fight. The burning rage is building inside of me, and I'm ready to tear Durin apart. As the thought pops into my mind, Durin walks through the front door.

Ethan stands up to greet him, and Marisa jumps across the room. She quickly makes her way toward me and stands behind me for protection. This is the first time she's been in the same room with the man she's been hunting for almost as long as she's been hunting me.

"What the hell is he doing here?" She hisses.

"I sent him a message asking him to come," Ethan confesses. "We need his help now more than ever."

"What kind of help is that?" I ask, looking straight at Ethan.

I'm afraid if I look directly at Durin, the urge to kill him will be too strong to fight any longer.

"We need you to help us, Reese," Durin explains, but I still can't bring myself to look at him. "For whatever reason, your emotions are controlling you. I don't understand why you want to kill me so badly. Before your accident, you were more than willing to help us take down Taltash."

"You better stop talking to me," I spoke through gritted teeth.

"You're the key to our success," he continued, "you're the only one that can get us inside. Once we're inside, there is nothing to stop us from ripping him and his operation apart."

"We need to unlock your memories," Ethan stepped in.

"I thought we could just wait for you to do it on your own, but it's clear to us now that you need help."

"I can give you the help you need." Durin stepped toward me, and it took all my strength not to attack him. "I have a method that can unlock all your memories, but you have to trust me."

"I can never trust you," I hissed in his face.

Marisa placed her hand on my arm, and Ethan stepped in front of me. I looked back at Marisa, and she smiled up at me. I glanced at Ethan, and he nodded reassuringly.

"We're here for you, Reese," Marisa whispered. "Ethan and I will make sure he doesn't do anything to you. I have my gun here, so you don't need to worry."

Ethan placed his hand on my shoulder and lifted my chin up so I could look into his eyes.

"You can trust us," he whispered.

I took a deep breath, stood up tall and proud, and nodded in agreement. I eyed Durin as he walked toward the middle of the room and knelt down. He gestured to the part of the floor across from him. Marisa squeezed my hand to give me courage. I squeezed back and then sat down in front of him.

"I need a knife for the process," Durin explained and looked up at Ethan.

Ethan pulled a small dagger from a hiding spot in his boot and handed it to him. I was ready to rip his hand off if he bought that knife too close to me.

He raised it to his own hand and slit the palm open. Then he flipped the knife around and handed me the hilt. He instructed me to do the same, and I did. The cut stung a little, but I'd suffered worse before.

He held his hand out toward me as the blood dripped from his cut to the ground.

"My blood is pure, and it will purge the blood of the demons within you," he explained slowly. "Our blood must mix for this to happen. Give me your hand."

I hesitated, but there was no point in backing out now. I held my cut hand out and grabbed his. Our cuts touched, and our blood mixed. His blood flowed into my veins, and I felt the burn as it spread through my body. I want to pull away, but his grip is strong, too strong for me to fight.

My memories flash through my mind, along with the memories of the demons within me. This time I can tell them apart. The memories that belong to me are stored away safely, and the memories that are not mine are thrown out of my mind. I fly past my memories inside my head, and in front of me, I can see the wall. The same wall I hit when I was with the witch doctor.

I try to pull away again, but I can't. The burning sensation is all over my body now. It feels like my blood is boiling inside of me. I'm melting from the inside out. The wall is getting closer, and I hit it. This time I go straight through it, and a big world opens up before me. All of my memories are mine again. I don't need to see them inside my head like the witch doctor and the hypnotist because I know they are mine.

It worked. I'm back. I'm me again. The demon blood is almost completely gone from my veins. The burn is getting stronger. I can't fight it, so I allow it to take over me. The wall is gone, and I know who put it there. I know why it was there. I know everything I need to know, but my hatred for Durin is still as strong as ever.

I know now why my hatred for him was never-ending. I understand why I need to end him. I know now that he killed my parents.

19

This Means War

My eyes snap open, and I take my first look at the new world in front of me. All my memories are there inside my head. I know exactly who I am and who I used to be. I know what needs to be done to both Durin and Taltash. I feel confident and strong. I feel like me.

I sit up and find myself in my bed. I look around, and everything seems both strange and familiar to me. I know this is my room, but the old me would never have stayed in a place like this. I can feel the demon blood still inside me, but it's my blood this time. I'm half-demon. That's okay, though, because now I'm strong enough to do what needs to be done.

I get up and get dressed. I'm not happy with the clothes I'm wearing. They're too casual, and the old me would never have worn them. I'm ready to go to battle, so I need to put on my battle clothes. I slid on the black stretchy jeans that hug my legs but still give me space to move. I put on a black tank top, and on top of that, I slid on my favorite leather jacket. I wouldn't wear leather because it makes too much noise, but what I'm about to do doesn't require stealth.

Once I'm ready, I exit my bedroom to see Marisa, Ethan, and Durin standing in my lounge. They look up at me. Each one of them has a different expression. Ethan and Marisa are a mixture of worried, although Ethan is worried and angry, Marisa is just worried. Durin is neutral. His face remains emotionless and unchanged.

I scan the room. Ethan is by the front door, and Marisa is in the kitchen. They're both far away from Durin, who is sitting on my couch. Neither of them is in a position to stop me.

I smile and blur across the room toward Durin. He jumps from the couch and prepares for my attack. He is fast, even faster than Ethan and I. I still manage to get my hand around his throat. He lifts his knee up into my stomach and chops his hand down on my arm, releasing his neck from my grip. I double over but quickly recover and spin round. I lift my leg up, and my foot collides with his chest sending him flying into the wall behind him. All this happens before Marisa and Ethan realize it.

Durin falls to the ground along with my small television, and Ethan blurs toward us. He grabs both my arms and pulls them behind my back. I grunt and groan as I try to pry myself free. Marisa is still frozen in the kitchen while her human brain works to decipher what is happening. We all moved too fast for her to see. She eventually runs over and helps Durin to his feet while I kick my legs out at him.

"What the hell, Reese!" Marisa yells as she lifts Durin up.

"Jesus Reese, do we have to put a leash on you?" Ethan muttered.

I continued to growl and kick at Durin while trying to pry myself free of Ethan's grip.

"Why did you do it, Durin?" I shouted and spat at him. "Why did you kill my parents?"

Durin's eyes grow wide, and Ethan lets go of me. I just about fly forward and stumble. I regain my composure and return my glare at Durin.

"What are you talking about?" He does an excellent job of faking confusion, but I'm not fooled.

"I remember now, Durin," I explained while baring my teeth. "That mental wall was put there by Taltash in case I was compromised. It would protect him from me, but it also protected you. I remember how you killed my parents because you wanted me to join your ranks. Taltash rescued me from you. You murdered them 22 years ago in Russia and took me from my home!"

"That's not true!" Durin is more angry than confused now. "You came to me because you discovered that Taltash was the one that killed your parents. You wanted to bring him down because of that."

"You're lying!"

"No, he's not," we all snap our heads in Marisa's direction. She walked off to grab her laptop and was now sitting on the kitchen floor. "I put in the dates. 22 years ago in Russia. Several people died that day, but only one married couple with a young daughter. The daughter was three years old and discovered missing after her parents were killed." She closed the laptop and looked up at me. "Durin wasn't even in Russia at the time. There are no signs of him or his men. Someone else was spotted in Russia at the same time as the murders, though."

She walked toward me and opened up the laptop. After I loaded, it showed a picture of my parents and me in an old Russian newspaper clipping. Beside the picture was an image of Taltash. He was in the country at the same time my parents were killed, and I went missing.

"If that's true," I muttered and took a deep breath. "Then why do my memories tell me differently? The night I died, I found out that Durin killed them."

"This is bad," Durin whispered. "This means that you weren't as trusted by Taltash as we suspected. That must be what the mental block was for. You realized that he killed your parents, so you came to us to help you get revenge. Taltash must have realized that you turned against him."

"He sent the men that killed you that night, and then he planted memories in your head," Ethan continued. "He must have suspected that we might try to bring you back using demon blood. He put protocols in place to protect himself."

"Taltash sounds kind of smart," Marisa swallowed hard.

"That's it," I lashed out and punched the wall next to me. "I'm sick and tired of people messing with my memories. We've got to take him down. I swear to God I will do everything I can to bring Taltash down."

"We need a plan first," Marisa interrupted.

Ethan grabbed me by the arm and pulled me away from the others. Marisa and Durin continued to discuss the plan while Ethan pulled me into the kitchen.

"So," he whispered, "are all your memories back? Do you remember us?"

I smiled at him as the memories became fresh in my mind. I remember him, and I remember us. I nod my head.

"I remember," I whispered back, but then my smile fades away. "I remember what we used to be, but I don't know if we can be that again. I'm not the same person you used to know."

He touched my cheek with the tips of his fingers. The sensation is warm and soft. I like it.

"That's okay. I think I like the person you are now, and I haven't changed. Do you still like the person I am?"

I smiled at him, but it was a sad smile of a forgotten past.

"I'll have to get back to you on that."

I pulled away from him and went back to the others. I tapped Marisa on the shoulder and gestured for her to follow me. I led her into my bedroom and slightly closed the door behind her.

"This is a little intimidating," she giggled. "Are you here to let me know that I've been the killer all along?"

"I'm sorry, Marisa," I started, but I wasn't sure how to finish the sentence. I swallowed hard and continued. "I know I sent you a lot of signals. Signals that might give off the impression that I want a relationship with you. Now that I have all my memories back, I don't know if I am deserving of that relationship anymore. If you knew the things I did, the person I used to be, I'm afraid you would be disgusted."

"It doesn't matter who you were." Marisa smiled up at me. It was an innocent and forgiving smile. "What matters is who you chose to be now. Besides, we can sort everything out once we're finished taking Taltash down."

I grinned, "That's what I like about you, straight to business." I sighed, and my face changed. "It's time to go to war."

20

Little Warrior

I HEADED TO TALTASH'S HEADQUARTERS ALONE. I KNEW exactly where I was going because I've been here at least a hundred times before. The entrance is guarded by random citizens and homeless people on the street. Each one of them would ask me a coded question. If I didn't answer correctly, they would sound the alarm, and this would all be over. It's a good thing I know all of the answers.

It's strange to have full control of my mind but to still feel like it is someone else's. I tried not to dwell on it.

"Why is the sky blue?" A man rushed toward me and asked.

The question was simple, even if it sounded strange. He is asking me why I've been quiet for so long.

"Because elephants eat bananas," I answer almost immediately. The answer I gave is that I was compromised and needed to lie low. I knew all the answers. They are all there in the back of my mind.

I kept walking, and a lady stepped forward to ask another question.

"Did the carrot fall asleep?" she asks me, which means am I still compromised.

"Only after the nuts sang their song," I replied instantly, informing her that I am no longer compromised.

The rest of them let me pass without any further questions. I reached the entrance to the tallest building in the city. I passed this building so many times before I had my memories. I couldn't believe that Taltash was in here the whole time. Two beefy guards are standing at the entrance to the building. They allow me to walk past. I expected them to stop me and search me for weapons. I am unarmed, but they aren't following routine. This worries me, but I continue to the elevator doors.

"Why does the sparrow fly south?" A small, skinny man asks me before allowing me to enter the elevator.

I smile, "He flies south because the winter approaches from the north."

The man lets me pass, and I enter the elevator. I press the button for the 50th floor and ride it all the way to the top of the building. I know that Taltash is waiting for me. I should have been checked for weapons before entering the building. The man should have asked me at least two questions, one before entering the elevator and one before allowing me to press the button for the top floor. Something is wrong. They aren't following procedure, but I can't dwell on that now. I need to focus on my job just as I know that Marisa, Ethan, and Durin are focusing on their jobs.

They have probably made their way into the building by now. They're getting into their positions, and I need to make sure I don't let them down.

The elevator doors open and I step out into a wide-open room. There are barely any walls in the room, only windows showing the blue sky outside and most of the city. The room is almost empty except for a few pieces of furniture and a big, old wooden desk at the end of the room. Taltash stood in front of the desk, with his hands behind his back. He looked straight at me as if he was ready for my arrival.

I looked at his face and remembered how much he used to mean to me. He raised me. He was a father to me, and even though those feelings for him are all but gone, I must pretend I still see him that way. I smiled the biggest smile I could manage and walked toward him.

"Father," I said as I raised my arms and opened them wide to wrap him in a hug. "I missed you."

I hugged him, but he didn't hug back. He pushed my arms down and pulled away from me. His face is twisted with anger, and there is a hint of distrust in his eyes.

"What is going on," he hissed at me. "I want answers! Tell me where you've been. Why have you been ignoring my messages? What happened at the gala, did you get cold feet? That's not like you."

"I had an accident," I explained to him as calmly as I would have before. "I lost my memories, and I was compromised. I've been working on getting them back."

He stared at me for what felt like ages.

"Have you got them back?"

I smiled and nodded in response. His face and eyes grew soft, with a genuine look of worry and relief. He wrapped his arms around me and pulled me in for a hug. I returned the hug and fought the urge to gag.

"I'm glad you're back," he whispered and kissed my head. "Now we can get started. I put my plans on hold because I didn't want to move forward without you."

He walked around his desk toward the wall of windows. I followed him and listened to what he has to say. I need to buy time for Marisa and Ethan. Marisa is trying to hack into Taltash's server and get all the information she can about all his operations. Ethan is working hard to get that information to Durin and his men. All I can do is buy them as much time as possible before completing my job.

"That politician we killed at the gala has already been replaced," Taltash explained. "He was the final piece. Now everything is in place, and we can move forward with our plans. We're going to level the poor districts of this city. Once the poorest areas are cleansed of the destitute and homeless, we can rebuild. We will build up this city like we have others and control it from the inside."

I listened to his plans, and they made me sick. This isn't how I usually feel, but my thoughts and feelings toward him changed when I discovered he killed my parents and stole me. I have to kill him. It's the best way to make sure his operation will come to an end and that he will never complete his plans.

Killing him won't be easy, though. He is immortal. I remember that much. Immortal demons are rare and almost impossible to kill. They use an old form of magic to place all of their mortal thoughts and feelings into one object. This object is personal to them, and by doing this, they make this object the very weapon that can kill them. Taltash never told me what his object was, but I always had an idea of it.

I glanced at the pen on his desk and hoped he was too distracted to notice. He bragged about the pen once to me. He bragged about how he had carved it out of the leg bone of the first man he killed, his brother. That's the most personal thing he owns, and he never lets anyone near it. If I had to guess, I would name it as the weapon that can kill him.

"Soon now, we will rule this cleansed and pure world together, my little warrior," he finished off his rant. He looked at me, expecting some kind of answer.

"Yes, Father," I said with a nod.

Something about the way I said it or what I said must have been wrong. His face turned sour, and he took a step back.

"Just how much of my daughter did I get back?" He asks. "You're different, Reese. I don't think you're my little warrior anymore. Are you?"

It's too late to save this. I lash out at him and blur toward the table to grab the pen. He blurs ahead of me and grabs my outstretched hand. Before I can grab the pen, he pulls my hand down, and the momentum flips my whole body over. I land on my back on top of his desk. I cough and spit, trying to regain some of the breath that was pushed out of my chest. Taltash reacted quickly and brought his flat hand down on my chest. I rolled over and blurred out of the position before he could. His hand cut straight through the desk, cutting it in half.

I followed the pen as it was flung across the floor. After seeing where it lands, I turned back to Taltash. He is strong and fast. More than anyone I have ever fought. If I hadn't died and been brought back with demon blood, he would have killed me in seconds. Now I stand a chance, but not much of one. My best bet is that pen.

Taltash didn't give me a second to recover. He kicked the one half of the desk in my direction. I flipped to the side to avoid it, but he kicked the second one too. I landed from my flip, and the second half of the desk collided with me. The force of his kick was great. The desk hit me, and I was sent flying along with it to the far wall.

My back slammed into the wall, and the air got knocked out of me. I didn't have time to catch my breath. Taltash blurred toward me. I kicked the desk back at him. It hit him and messed up his trajectory. He ended up running straight into the wall next to me. I eyed the pen on the floor and tried to think of a way to get to it.

I spun round to meet Taltash. I lashed my flat hand at his face and kicked my leg out at his stomach. I moved as fast as I could, but he was still faster than me. He blocked and pushed away both my attacks. He lashed his own fist out at me, but I pushed away from the wall, and he ended up punching it instead. I did a backflip to get away from him, but also to get closer to the pen. As my feet touched the ground, I spun around and got down on my knees. I grabbed the pen and wrapped my fingers around it completely so he couldn't see it.

He was behind me now. He dug his fingers into my shoulder, lifted me up, and turned me around to face him. He raised his arm up above my head and prepared to bring it down on my face. I clicked the pen, pulled my arm across my chest, and thrust my hand upward into his chest.

He gasped as the pen pushed through his skin. It was lodged in his flesh, and I pulled my hand away. I straightened my other hand and thrust my open palm against the back of the pen with all my strength. The pen pressed deeper into his body and impaled his heart—the only way to kill an immortal demon.

He froze for only a second, and then his arms dropped to his side, and he stumbled backward. His knees grew weak and collapsed beneath him. He brought his hands to his chest to cradle the bleeding wound. Black blood flooded out of the small hole in his chest and pooled across the floor. He looked down with wide eyes, unwilling to believe it was possible. He looked back up at me, and I could see the shock of my betrayal in his eyes.

"Why," he gasped and choked. "Why have you done this to me, daughter?" He spat out some blood and coughed. "I raised you as my own. I made you who you are."

I walked toward him and knelt down in front of him. I looked straight into his eyes, and my face was cold and hard.

"I know you killed my parents," I whispered. "I don't know why you did it, but I know that you wanted me for some reason. You killed my parents, and you stole me. You tried to blame it on Durin."

I had more to say, but he started chuckling even though each movement and sound he made was painful.

"But you're too smart for that," he struggled to speak and breathe. "I knew you were more. You're going to be powerful one day, and I'm only sad I won't be here to see that day."

I stood up and used my foot to push him over. He rolled onto the ground, and the life left his dark eyes. He let out his last breath, and that was it. It's over now. I won the battle and killed the immortal demon, but the war will go on after his death.

I remembered something that I wanted. Something that Taltash took away from me a long time ago. My eyes are drawn to an old, wooden box on the shelf near the wall. The box is engraved with runes from an old and forgotten language. I walk over and open the box. Inside is the pendant. It belonged to my mother, her mother before her, and her mother's mother before. It's been in my family for such a long time. Now it belongs to me. I lift it out of the box and place it around my neck, and all feels right with the world.

I don't know why, but Taltash wanted this pendant for something. I take a moment to admire it. It's a flat piece of gold, like a coin, with a single rune carved into it. I don't know what the rune means, but it is the same language that is carved into the box. Taltash stole me and this pendant for a reason. One day I'll find out what that reason is, but for now, I have this small piece of my family back, and I won't let his memory taint it.

My job is done here, and I can leave. I make my way out of the building. It was full and busy when I arrived, and now it is empty and quiet. All of Taltash's men must have had jobs to do. They had instructions to carry out if ever he was defeated. Now they have disappeared to carry out those instructions.

Outside the building, Marisa is waiting for me with the entire police department. I walk toward her sporting my family pendant and holding my head up with a new feeling of pride.

"How is everything going?" I ask her.

"We're still downloading information from the servers, but one of Taltash's men must have flipped a switch or something," Marisa explained as she walked me through the police crowd. "One moment we're downloading everything, and it's going well, the next thing we know, the information is getting deleted. Someone put a virus in the system, and now we're racing to download everything we can."

"Taltash's men were given instructions," I explained. "They had jobs to do in the case of his death. All the plans were put into place the moment I killed him. This is a big battle that we've won, but the war will keep going on."

"She means that killing Taltash only opened up a spot for the next big bad guy to step into." Ethan walked into the scene like he owned it, and he had Durin in tow.

"I managed to extract some information about whoever is supposed to take Taltash's place. We can track them down one by one," he looked into my eyes and smiled, "together."

I nodded my head in agreement and returned his smile. I turned to Durin and gave him a glare that he wouldn't soon forget.

"I still don't trust you, Durin," I growled. "I don't care if you weren't the one that killed my parents. Something about you is off, and I will never trust you. In fact, if I see you again, I might just have to kill you."

Ethan looked back at Durin with shock, but Durin just grinned.

"I'll keep that in mind," he replied softly and calmly. "Come, Ethan, we have work to do. You can see your pet later."

Durin walked away, and Ethan hesitated to follow. He looked to me for guidance, and I gave him a reassuring nod. I know I'll see him again. We still have a future together. I'm not sure what kind of future it is, though. All I know is that I'm really looking forward to taking down the rest of Taltash's operations, and I know he'll be by my side.

I turned back to Marisa. She had her hands busy, typing like a mad person on her laptop. I watched her for a while until she realized that I was. She glanced up at me, and I spotted a grin pulling at her lips before she returned her eyes to the laptop screen.

"Take a picture, it will last longer," she mumbled.

"How about I buy you a drink instead," I replied as I leaned against the hood of the police car she was using as a table.

She tried to hide the excitement in her eyes as she nodded in response and continued her work.

It seems my life is getting back to normal. I fought my demons, and I won. Now I have to make sure it stays this way.

About the Author

Renee Joiner has been in love with the supernatural for longer than she can remember, so it is no surprise that she is an author of paranormal urban fantasy. Although she discovered her passion for writing when she was only twelve years old, she didn't make her writing debut until many years into the future. Adventurous and fun-loving, she enjoys traveling to new places, exploring new sights and meeting new people. Thus, she delights in creating fantastical worlds that are sure to give her readers an escape from the real world while simultaneously providing thrilling entertainment.

Besides her special knack for writing, you'll also find a passion for metaphysics spirituality which she has been nurturing for over four decades. Renee hails from New York and currently resides with her husband in their empty nest—unless you count their three adorable fur babies—in Florida. She enjoys adding to her sea of knowledge and thus spends her free time learning new things.

To find out more about Renee Joiner, feel free to visit her **official website**.

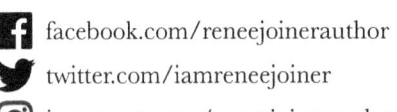

facebook.com/reneejoinerauthor

twitter.com/iamreneejoiner

instagram.com/reneejoinerauthor

More Books by Renee

Single

Tempest

Dark Huntress Series

Glen Cove

The Witch

The Djinn

The Countess

Magic of the Night Series

Raven Magic

Thank You...

Thank you for reading my book!

I really appreciate all of your feedback and I love to hear what you have to say. Please leave your review at your favorite retailer!